Angel Wing Splash Pattern

Richard Van Camp

Kegedonce Press
Cape Croker Reserve
R.R. 5 Wiarton, Ontario
Canada N0H 2T0

Angel Wing Splash Pattern

Sixth printing, 2012

Cover and Book Design: Rockpaperscissors
Cover Image: © 2002 Tim Atherton
Editor: Kateri Akiwenzie-Damm

Kegedonce Press
Cape Croker Reserve
R.R. 5 Wiarton, Ontario, Canada N0H 2T0
Phone: 519 371-1434   Fax: 519 371-5011
Email: renee@kegedonce.com and kateri@kegedonce.com
Website: www.kegedonce.com

Van Camp, Richard, 1971 - 2nd ed.
Angel wing splash pattern/Richard Van Camp.—2nd ed.

ISBN-10 0-9731396-0-9   ISBN-13 978-0-9731396-0-0

    1. Indians of North America - Canada - Fiction. I. Title.
PS8593.A5376A75 2002   C813,.54   C2002-903786-7
PR9199.3.V356A75 2002

Kegedonce Press gratefully acknowledges the support of the
Canada Council for the Arts and the Ontario Arts Council.

The Canada Council | Le Conseil des Arts
for the Arts | du Canada

ONTARIO ARTS COUNCIL
CONSEIL DES ARTS DE L'ONTARIO

Distributed by Lit-Distco
100 Armstrong Avenue
Georgetown, Ontario
Canada L7G 5S4
Tel: 1.800.591.6250 Fax: 1.800.591.6251 Email: orders@litdistco.ca

Member of Cancopy

Printed and bound in Canada by Hume

In memory of my grandfather,

Pierre Wah-shee

Contents

angel wing

Mermaids

Come flying out of the Range Hotel. Elbow's busted. Bleeding through my sock. Gotta find those sisters. Right rump is sore. Took the fall so I wouldn't go through the TV. Yellowknife. I hate this town. Cabbies everywhere. The little Native girl I saw waiting earlier is still there. Waiting. Still waiting. For who—her folks? She's got those yellow gumboots on. Christ, she's gotta be cold. It's late. What time is it? Gotta make that bus. I feel my blood drain and pool in my boot. I head towards her. Her face is filthy. She's shivering. I gotta make that bus.

"You're bleeding," she says.

I lean hard against a parking meter. "You should be inside."

"I can stay out late as I want," she insists.

My throat. Everything starts spinning. My mother was cursed. I swallow blood. The day she bore me. I stare at the little girl and I am faint with envy of the dead. "Did I ever tell you why God killed the mermaids?"

That's when I black out.

When I come to, I'm in an apartment. Awful little apartment. Black velvet paintings on the wall. Sticky beer on the kitchen floor. Something sticky all over me. Band-Aids. I got Barbie Band-Aids on my arms and hands. All over my throat and face. There's a party next door. I'm sitting down with my sock off. Did she drag me here? She comes around the corner holding something.

"What you got there?"

"My last Band-Aid," she says, "for your foot."

I look down. The skin on the back of my foot is torn absolutely off. It's stopped bleeding. Lint and hair on my pink wound.

"Okay," I say.

She rolls the Band-Aid on while I wiggle my toes. "Don't pick it," she says.

I look around. I'm sitting on urea foam furniture. Christ, these people. Don't they know anything?

"Don't pick it," she warns. "Don't pick it. Don't pick it."

"Where's your mom?"

"Working."

"Yeah right," I say. "This late?"

She crosses her arms. "My mom's working."

"Okay, kid, okay. You're the boss. Does your mom have any smokes around here, or what?"

Shakes her head. What kind of Indian is she? "Are you Cree, Chip or Slavey?"

"I'm Dene. Why did God kill the mermaids?"

"Come on," I say. "You don't want to know why God killed them."

"Sure I do," she says. Before I know it, she sits on my knee. I think I chipped the blade of my elbow off. I can't seem to move it. Legs are tightening up too. Who would have guessed I could kick them so far forward?

"How old are you?" I ask.

"Nine," she says.

My meds. Good thing I take my meds. I can miss two meals and never feel it cuz I take my meds.

"What happened to your arms?" she asks.

My tattoos. She's covered my tattoos with Barbie Band-Aids.

2

I smoldered them off with a car lighter after Sfen died. They were home-grown crosses Sfen gimme, one on each arm. "Accident," I said. "What's your name?"

"Stephanie. What's yours?"

"You never heard of me?"

She shakes her head. She's gonna be pretty with those dark eyes of hers. She's gotta be Slavey.

"You sure?" I look around. "My name's Torchy."

"That's not your name," she says.

"Sure it is."

"What's your real name?"

I look around again. No one here but us. "Hazel," I said. "But I hate that name. Call me Torchy."

"Why do they call you Torchy?"

"You don't want to know."

Her eyes light up. "Sure I do."

"Because I like to burn things down," I say.

"Why?"

"I got a gene variant."

"A what?"

"A cocaine gland in my brain. It spills sometimes."

She frowns. "Don't lie."

"Hey. How does God clean?"

"With his hands."

"No. He cleans with fire. And I would rather unleash fire than have fire unleash me."

She didn't get it. She didn't even hear me. She pouts her lips. "But firebugs pee their bed."

"What?"

"My daddy told me firebugs pee their bed."

I laugh for the first time in months. "Where's your old man?"

She doesn't answer. Looks down. I shoulda known better.

"Why did God kill the mermaids, Torchy?"

"God killed the mermaids," I say. "He did, you know."

She looks at me with a filthy face. Rests her little head on my bony shoulder. "But why?"

Jesus, this kid trusts me. Doesn't she know who I am? Eleven o'clock at night. Her folks are drinkin' and she's here with me. Okay. She saved me so maybe I owe her. I need time. Need to power up. It's eleven now. I gotta make that midnight bus.

"Well," I say, "this is a story. It's not an old time story. It's not a 'Once upon a Time' story. It's a Torchy story and—Christ—I wish your mom had a smoke around here. I can feel my brain swelling."

"Torchy—"

"Okay. Okay. The best I can figure is when sailors saw the mermaids, they leapt from their boats and swam to them. They forgot about their houses, their mortgages, their ol' ladies, they forgot about all that. They saw such beautiful women. They just wanted to be with them. And if they died swimming across, they died with glory in their eyes. Then they saw the mermen. While they were swimming. These mermen were so beautiful they fell in love with them, too. They became bi-sexual."

I look at the little girl for her reaction. She's listening but she's got sleepy eyes.

"You know what that means?" She shakes her head. "That means you love everyone and everything around you. You love men.

You love women. You love puppies and you love Country and Western music. You just love everything. And everyone. The mermaids and mermen were so beautiful, the men wanted to stay there forever until they died. They carved temples out of Chinese jade for them, so the mermaids and mermen could sit on altars. The mermen would have to remind the men to eat. They were so in love they forgot to eat. Like the bison when they're rutting. They forget to eat, eh? They just wanted love."

I look. She's almost asleep. "God killed the mermaids because they were more beautiful than God. Men worshipped mermaids and mermen. They forgot about God and anytime men forget about God, He reminds them that He's still there. That's why he brought AIDS. Because we forgot."

I flex my fingers. Make a fist. Oh, I'm gonna feel this all tomorrow. I lean back in the chair. I hope my throat doesn't close. I hold Stephanie close. She's still got those gumboots on. I hug her and hold her close.

"Where do fish sleep?" she asks suddenly.

"I thought you were sleeping. What?"

"Where do fish sleep?"

"I don't know."

She smiles. "On river beds, silly."

"Oh," I say. Then we burst out laughing.

She studies me deep. "Are you a bad man, Torchy?"

I think about this long and hard. "Am I a bad man?" I ask. "I'm not a bad man. I just leave for a while and let the bad man in."

I think of another logo me and Sfen could have done if he would have met this little girl. It would say, LAUGHTER IS THE BEST

MEDICINE and under it we could have little kid's handwriting that says: AND HUGS HELP TOO.

They used to call my brother "the idea man." He was a logo artist by trade, but I couldn't think about that. I lift Stephanie and place her on the sofa. Where's Stephanie's mom? Doesn't she know guys worse than me walked the streets? Some guys right now would be pullin' their junk lookin' at her.

How much money do I got left? Four hundreds. There's a red crayon. Good. I take it and write on each bill, "My mother was cursed the day she bore me. I am faint with envy of the dead."

I look out the window to the Yellowknife sky. I love how clouds here fold themselves and burn for sunsets. I pray, I guess, in my own way. Bless these bills, someone. May each of these bills burn to sunlight. May each of these bills change lives forever, for good.

How'm I gonna explain this to Snowbird? The old man who blessed my hands and warned me, "Grandson," he said, "make sure you drop some tobacco when you get to Yellowknife. Say your name out loud after you land so your soul can catch up with you and don't forget to wash your hands after you win."

It was only yesterday when I worked up the courage to go see him.

"Old man?" I called as I walked into his porch.

"A-mi-nay?" he asked. "Who's there?"

"Maybe I'm your long lost grandson, and maybe I want to make my long lost grandpa rich."

The medicine man called Snowbird studied me with glassy, filmy eyes. It looked like someone had emptied an egg into each of his sockets. We were quiet for a bit. I recognized the music on the radio.

It was Van Morrisson's "Sometimes I feel like a motherless child." It was a hurtin' song so we listened hard.

He opened the door of his wood stove with a piece of fresh kindling, and popped a large spruce in before closing the door with the same stick. He waved the glowing stick around in the air and I could smell its beautiful sweet smoke.

"I remember you when you were this high," he lifted his brown hand to his knee. "Hey-ya-hay!" the old man smiled, "I better put on some tea so me and my long lost grandson can catch up. Also, we should pray now that we have found each other after all these years."

Snowbird must have been the loneliest man in the world, the way he moved. He pulled out a pouch of Drum and opened his wood-stove. He threw in a pinch of tobacco and began to pray in Dogrib. I was disgusted with how lonely he was. He was starving for someone to talk to. I watched him pray and didn't understand a word. He then switched to English: "...and this is for my adopted grandson," he said. Then he handed the pouch to me. "Now you, Grandson."

I pinched some tobacco and pulled it out. "For everyone with AIDS," I said.

"Ho," he said.

I threw the tobacco to the naked fire. It smelled sweet.

"For my brother Sfen."

"Ho."

I was just about to cross myself but suddenly remembered: "For all my enemies."

"Ho!" he said really loud. Maybe I was praying for us both.

"I'm sorry to hear, Grandpa," I said, "that your wife died."

"Yes yes," he answered sadly, "but that is God's plan. Not ours. It's up to the boss upstairs." He pointed with the piece of kindling to the ceiling. "Jesus was a medicine man."

"Here are the signs," he said as he sucked on his pipe. "There are three wolves running outside of town. Three wolves. One is white. One is gray. One is black. Wolves are how the Creator moves over the snow."

I thought of lepers and tornadoes touching down.

He was quiet for a while before he said, "There is talk of a midnight burial outside of town, by the lake."

I cleared my throat but couldn't speak. Don't ask about my brother, I was thinking. Don't you dare ask about my brother.

He waited a long, long time before saying with a soft voice, "That's all right, grandson. We do what we have to, don't we?"

I nodded, waited for the tears to stop burning my eyes. How did he know? I waited, nodded again, looked away. How did he know? He poured us some tea and turned the radio off.

"Why have you come here, Grandson?"

I took a big breath. "I want the jackpot in tomorrow's Bingo in Yellowknife. Eighty grand cash. I'll give you half if you bless my hands with your medicine."

He thought about it. Nodded. "Come visit your grandpa tomorrow before you leave," he said.

Great! "But I have to get on the plane. Will it last until Yellowknife?"

"Yes. Just don't touch any cards or Bingo dabbers until you get to the game you want to win."

"What if we have to share the pot with someone in Y.K?"

"You won't."

I waited. "What will you do with your half, old man?"

He was quiet for even longer. It was like he was listening to the fire and remembering the words of the song and each instrument in the band and maybe the thoughts of each band player and mister Van himself. It was as if he realized again how pitiful he was hugging such loneliness every day. "Do you know what I wish?" he asked. "I wish someone were to visit me and read to me the Bible. It is such a beautiful song sung with so many voices. I could make tea and we could talk after. That's what I wish, grandson."

I stood up. Me? He was talking about me.

"I don't want money," he continued. "You're young. You keep it. But please remember your Grandpa."

A medicine man saying please to me. I couldn't believe it. He held out his small, brittle hand. I took it. It was almost like his fingers were made with the same tiny hollow bones in sparrow wings.

"Is there a woman in your life, Grandson? Where are all my grandchildren?"

I remembered me and Sfen sneaking out to the highway at night to hunt ptarmigan sitting high in the poplars. "There's no such thing as '90's love," I said and pushed away. "The earth is burning, Grandpa."

"Why do you talk like this?"

I looked into his blind eyes. "It's gonna take hell for me to find another heart that beats like mine."

He nodded. Didn't know what the hell I was talking about.

"I have to go, Grandpa."

"Come visit me tomorrow," he said. "I'll bless your hands."

I coughed I would. "Grandpa," I said. "Can I ask you a question?"

"That's what grandpas are for."

"Why don't you cure yourself? Your eyes, I mean."

He worked his tight little lips around his fake teeth. "I would have to kill a man and take his eyes," he said. "Then where would I be? I just have to tap my cane and children take me where I wish to go. If I could see, they would not help me anymore. I am already in heaven, Grandson. You were the one who could smell the fireweed roots, weren't you?"

That's right! I had forgotten. I remembered taking the old man's cane and leading him to the Bay when I was a child.

"What do you smell, Grandson?" he would ask.

"Fire," I'd answer. "I smell fire."

He would chuckle deep into his chest. I could smell fire even when I was a little boy, and I could smell cancer in trees. So how did I end up bloody in Yellowknife with blessed hands? I won the Bingo game, all right, just like the old man said I would. I had eighty thousand dollars cash in two duffel bags. I should have put it in storage, but I ended up taking a taxi right to the top of the Gold Range. I figured the old man's medicine could win me more. It did. I won every hand I played: Blackjack, Poker. I got the Gook who ran the place to bring me some ginger pork and rice. And then I saw the hookers, two Gook sisters who wanted me, so I bought a room, but I forgot to wash my hands.

I woke up choking after throwing fire into both twins. I was being choked. I looked for someone to kill. No one. There was no one I could see, then I realized they were my own hands choking off my windpipe. The twins shot up screaming. My own hands were killing me. I couldn't breathe. I was gagging so I charged to the bathroom.

I knew what was happening. The old man's medicine ran out and turned sour. I sat down and pulled my legs back and kicked my arms loose. That's when I saw them. I had claws instead of hands. The devil's claws were on me. The same hands that won me eighty grand plus were digging through my throat. But I got the tub going. I got it going and I put those claws under the bloody water for a long time until they turned back to my hands. When I went back to the room, the twins had vanished with all my money.

I remembered the night Sfen told me everything. We were at the Lake. It was such a pretty night for sin. We were relaxing after kicking in the door and looting the Warden's house. Sfen knew the Warden was in the city with his ol' lady. And just like the song, there was a smoke on the water. There were parties rocking hard across the lake. Sitting around our fire, counting stars, trying to make out the voices, we strained to hear what they were talking about.

"This is my favorite place in the whole world, brother," he said.

I thought about it. "Mine too, I guess."

We could hear ducks laugh with wooden throats somewhere not too far away. A few mallards whistled by overhead. There was a breeze then, the first breeze of summer. It was cool and it whispered through the hair on our arms. We shared the Warden's smokes, passed the Warden's bottle. That's when Sfen told me everything.

But I had known a long time ago. The way his skull sucked his face in. The night sweats that drenched his mattress.

I should have asked the old man if he had medicine for AIDS. What animal would know which part of itself to give? The caribou? I heard the cure for cancer is in the root of a bear's tongue. But which part, and which cancer? There are so many now.

"What am I gonna do, Torch?" Sfen asked. He had lost so much weight the last year. He couldn't stop his hands from shaking and he wiped his tears away with his sleeve. "It's getting worse every day. I can't take it anymore and I don't want to take it anymore."

I tried so hard to think of the perfect answer and it suddenly hit me we were sharing the same bottle and the same cigarette. Could you get AIDS from that?

"What would a wolf do?" I asked Sfen.

"That isn't the question," Sfen said. "What would a sick wolf do? I have AIDS, Torchy. I'm dying. I ran outta my pills yesterday and I ain't going to the drug store in town. If anyone finds out, Torch, we're both dead and you know it. We ain't exactly town heroes."

"You're out of meds? Sfen, you need those. What are we doing here then? Christ, we should make a run to the city and get some more."

I started shaking. Something was up. That's when he said, "You know, Torch, I been thinking. All my furniture is stuffed with that urea foam. You told me once it releases cyanide gas when it burns."

I stood up and yelled, "What are you talking like this for!?"

"I'd sit up when I heard the fire alarm," he continued. "You'd have to do it when I was asleep. I'd sit up and breathe two lungs full. It'd be painless, wouldn't it? You'd do that for me wouldn't you?"

"No!" I said. "Never! Sfen don't talk like that!" And that's when I ran. I ran all the way up the road as far as I could. I ran until I puked. I was thinking this wasn't happening. I kept waiting for someone to tell me this wasn't real. I was thinking until I couldn't think any more and that's when I heard the shot.

The Warden's gun.

The one we found under the bed. The one I was gonna take back to town and stash.

On the beach. There was blood everywhere when I found him. My brother's eyes were still open. I never seen blood so red. The Warden's rosary braided through his fingers. Sfen's eyes wide open. Looking at the lake. I never seen blood so red.

And there was his cigarette. Still smoking. Blowing itself away.

I picked it up, finished it all by myself. The party didn't even stop across the lake. People just hooted and cheered when they heard the shot.

Now Sfen is where the fish sleep. At the lake, by the river bed. My brother who loved mermen.

"Torchy? Torchy!" Stephanie is shaking me. "Torchy? You were having a nightmare."

I look around, covered in sweat. "I was?"

"You were calling for Sfen. Who's Sfen?"

I look down. "My brother."

"Where is he? Is that who you were looking for?"

"Yeah," I wipe my sleeve across my eyes, "but he's gone."

"Just like my daddy's gone," she says. "My mom says he was fast. Faster than the wind. He froze to death, she says. Maybe the wind caught him." She looks at me and says, "I'll be your sister, Torchy, if you'll be my brother."

I can feel it build. I don't want to scare her so I move fast and picked her up. I hug her and I start to cry. I have to keep it quiet but I can't stop.

"Take me with you, Torchy," she says. "I don't want to stay here anymore. I'm scared all the time. I'll wash floors. I'll cook. I'll clean…"

I think of the old man and I look at my hands. "Do you want to come with me? To where I live?"

She looks around. "What about my mom?"

"We'll call your mom when things get better, okay? There's a bus leaving in half an hour to Simmer. There's an old man I want you to meet—my grandpa. He really wants to meet you."

She scratches her head and smiles. "He does?"

"Yeah," I say. "He does. Can you read?"

She nods. "Let's go, Torchy. Let's go to your home."

I remembered Sfen, when we were kids. One of my mom's boyfriends felt guilty, I guess, for beating on all of us. He took us to the lake after for a picnic of chips and beer. He also bought one pair of flippers for me and Sfen.

Mom needed shades to hide the love he put on her. "You're gonna have to learn to share," she called weakly as we ran from the car. "You two are brothers and brothers share."

"It's okay, Torchy," Sfen whispered. "Don't look at him."

Sfen's left eye was swollen shut. He had to help me with mine because my arms were so sore. I got the right flipper because I had smaller feet. He took the left, though it was too tight for him. We held hands and ran to the water. The same lake I buried him beside. We ran together, my big brother and me, never letting go, laughing, free…

Let's Beat the Shit Out of Herman Rosko!

"Look at Kevin Costner," Clarence added, standing in his jack boots and camouflage pants.

"Kevin Costner. What about him?"

He waved his hands in the air. "The Indians always save Kevin Costner. There was Dances with Wolves and Revenge. "

I thought about it. "Revenge? That was the Mexicans that saved him."

"Cousins!" Clarence cried. "The Mexicans are our cousins."

"Robin Hood and Bull Durham didn't have any Indians in them."

"The system, Grant," he shook his head, "the Wonder Breads are keeping us down. Look at this street: Little Vietnam. Look at this place: Row housing. When the CF-18's are carpet bombing the revolution, they'll just have to make one swoop and this town'll go up."

We were quiet and bowed our heads. We had been standing on the street outside Herman's house for quite some time now.

"Now let's go git him!" He urged.

"Now? Let's go for jav."

Clarence tossed his long black hair. "You know what he told Duane?"

"Duane? Duane with the new shoes?"

"Yeah—you know what he told him?"

I sat down near the ditch. "What?"

"He told Duane," Clarence flicked his cigarette ash with his fingernail, "you either marry or your mom or your dad."

I had to shield my eyes from his brand new chequered cowboy shirt to look at him. I thought of my mom. I loved my mom. I thought of my dad. I loved him too. "So?"

Clarence kicked a stone into the ditch. "What is he teaching anyway?"

"Marriage counseling," I answered. "He's a sex therapist, too."

Clarence shook his head. "The guy goes to university and he thinks he's Gandhi."

I eyed Herman's house while Clarence shook his head and she didn't look good. The lawn was a symphony of leaves and the house looked crooked. Herman's whole property boasted machine silence. There were three fading Buicks in the driveway that hadn't seen action in years, one of which had a safety pin head dress hanging from the rear view mirror. There were two dusty washers and a dryer under the walk-way. Next to an oil-drum, there was an old ten speed lying on the lawn: wheels pretzeled, forks bent.

Clarence made a fist and spat. "We kicked his ass in elementary and we kicked his ass in high school. Let's gear down and go get him."

"Now wait up," I said, handing him another cigarette.

Clarence took the smoke and stuck it behind his ear. A cloud of sandflies sprayed their way out like a black halo before charging back into his hair. We looked to the left and heard a truck guzzling through town. "All right," Clarence smiled. "The man."

Brutus and his monster truck bounced their way through the potato field. The tarp on the back of his truck came loose and a couple caribou legs flew out. Old Man Johnson's dogs chained in the bush behind us started howling *arooo arooo*.

"That truck was customized to break every noise by-law in town," Clarence grinned. There was a mosquito on his chin; its belly glowed like red sap hardened by the sun.

"Who'd have the ka-ho-nees to give him a ticket?" I asked.

Brutus flashed his brights. I could see the rifle rack behind his head. His truck growled and roared directly towards us. It wasn't really win-win negotiation. All I could do was stay still and pray his break fluid wasn't low. From the closing distance, I saw Brutus' silver Highway Patrol glasses and that smile, that barracuda smile, cradled by a handlebar moustache.

"Shiiiiiiiiiiiiit," was all I could say as he and that muscle truck got closer and closer.

SQWAKKKKKK!!

The fender was a splash parade of flapping dragonflies, mosquito pepper and a dislocated sparrow wing. The truck gadug gadug gadug'd as it idled. His polar bear license plate read "BALLS." We could hear Willie Nelson calling through his nose like a moose for someone to help him make it through the night. Brutus shut'er down and ran his fingers through his long brown hair. His python arms were flexed as he wore his "Don't Worry Be Hopi" muscle T-shirt that we stole off some kid's snowman two years ago. Leaning out his window and craning his neck, he eyed Herman's house.

"Boys," he nodded. "Whatchooupto? Who's got a smoke for Uncle?" Clarence eyed the smokes in my right shirt pocket.

"I only got two left 'til payday," I said.

It was Tuesday. Payday was next week.

"Quit yer bitchin'," Brutus said, "ya mooch."

He took my smoke. "Who's got fire?"

I, like always, lit it for him. He leaned into it and took a long puff and blew a white plume out for all of us to see.

"You dropped a couple of hindquarters," I pointed out.

"Blood shot anyways," Brutus said.

"That's a waste," Clarence said, "in traditional times blood-shot meat was good for soup. In traditional times our elders used to—"

"When was the last time you hunted?" Brutus asked. Clarence stopped short and was quiet.

"Well, the dogs'll be happy," I tried. "They'll eat good tonight."

"Where's Kevin?" Clarence asked. "I thought you were going to bring him."

Brutus eyed him. "Is your ass itchy?"

Clarence frowned. "No."

"Well, I guess he ain't up there, now is he?" Brutus smiled and winked at me. "He's watching the hockey game—Hey!" He pointed back to Clarence. "You got a hair eater on your back!"

"What!" Clarence said, "Where!?"

"On your back!" Brutus screamed. "It's on your fuckin' back!"

"Fuck — holy fuck — fuck that fuckin' bug!" Clarence yelled hopping and spinning around.

"SPRUCE BEETLE!" Brutus hollered the alarm of doom.

"Fuckin' hair eaters!" I yelled. I saw the spruce beetle's thick black back as big as my thumb and its six insectoid legs, just plastic and shiny, boy. He was locked on and wouldn't move.

"Look at the tentacles on that thing!" Brutus screamed. "They're bigger'n my cock!"

"Get him off me! Get him off me!" Clarence whirled and slapped himself. He ran and leaned right into me. "Get him off meeee!!"

I shot up and ran away. "Fuck you!" I yelled. "GET AWAYYYYYYYY!!"

I ran into Herman's yard. Brutus rolled up his window. I couldn't see where Clarence was but I could hear his big black boots clomping across the street. I could see Brutus laughing away, his head back, his black molar fillings. There was no sound, just his walrus moustache shivering, his Adam's apple bobbing.

I ran around the side of the truck to watch Clarence whip down on the grass and start doing the crab walk on his back. Old Man Johnson's dogs started howling again: *Aroooooo! Aroooo!*

I walked over to the truck. Brutus rolled down his window. "You gonna beat up Herman?" I asked.

"Negative," he wiped his eyes, "guy taught me how to use four cubes of ice on Iris."

I thought about it. "Four ice cubes?"

"Can't say, little buddy."

"Why?"

"Code of conduct, man. Herman's a sexual ninja who teaches only those who are ready."

"Well I'm ready."

Brutus looked at me. "Talk does not cook rice."

Clarence came back dusting himself off. "Traitors," he pouted. "You fuckin' guys."

The sandflies were at his ears again and the fat mosquito was gone, probably straight to the swamp to reproduce and die.

"Sure you got him?" Brutus said.

Clarence looked at him sideways. "Pretty fuckin' sure."

"Hear about the yellow Halls?" Brutus asked. "Herman's got a cure for Indians who won't go down."

"The what?"

"Shit," Clarence said. "Shit, that Herman!"

"What's the deal with the yellow Halls?"

"Guy's pretty smart," Brutus grinned. "The Northern's already sold out."

"Well what the hell is it?" I asked. I wanted to know about the four ice cubes and I wanted to know about the yellow Halls!

Clarence helped himself to my last smoke. He looked pretty pissed off so alls I could do was look at the one behind his ear and shake my head. He was so mad he didn't even smoke it. He just slid it behind his other ear for later.

"Get this," Brutus said and turned his truck off. "Herman," he took a puff, "Herman says if you don't usually go down on your woman, just use yellow Halls."

"Yellow Halls?"

"With the menthol liptis?"

Brutus nodded, "That's right, you know—for colds."

"What about them?"

"You put them in your mouth and go down on your woman. It's great." I thought about it. Clarence did too.

"Doesn't it burn?" I asked.

"Fuck sakes. Now he's telling us how to lick our women!"

"Herman says it makes the petals of a woman blush."

Clarence slapped his neck. "The guy's a fuckin' poet too?"

"He said it's okay to hum the national anthem when you go down—or Hockey Night in Canada. The chicks love it!"

"Well you know what I heard?" Clarence asked with a red face. "I heard when you go down on a woman it's like suckin' the dick of every man who's ever been there."

Brutus and I looked at Clarence with horror. I watched the nipple of mosquito itch rising on Clarence's neck. I turned to Brutus. "Is he still seeing Renee?"

"She's seeing Jon now."

"Big Jon?"

"Quiet Jon."

"So he's single?"

"And loving it. I heard Tanya stayed over there last night."

"Shit," Clarence slapped his legs. "Shit!"

Bingo. That's why we were here. Tanya used to shack up with Clarence who stood now with his hands in his pockets.

"Maybe you should have beat the shit out of her, Clarence," Brutus smiled. "Lord knows she'd never've left you."

Clarence and I stared at Brutus in disbelief until he smiled. "Wah!"

"I say we go in there and stomp his ass," Clarence said. "Dogs understand three things: war, meat, and fucking. We're Dogrib: It's in our blood. He's a Rosko; he'll always be a Rosko. Just cuz he went to university don't make him any different. It'll be just like old times, tradition. Let's go trauma-hawk him."

"Fuck you guys," Brutus started his truck. "I'm going home to skin some rats. You wanna help?"

Clarence and I wrinkled our faces.

"Thought so," Brutus said.

BAROOOOOOOOOOOOMMM!!

The truck glowed as it hit reverse. The black exhaust found us. I coughed and I hacked. Brutus reached in his glove compartment and threw something at us. It was two packs of yellow Halls.

He put it in gear. "Sol later, mooches. See you at baseball, Sunday."

We both looked to our hands as Brutus sped off down the street.

"Citrus," I read aloud. We were quiet for a bit. I unwrapped mine and put one in my mouth.

"So, cousin," Clarence said, "are we gonna rock and roll?"

"In a minute," I waved, blowing my breath against my palm. "Time is it?"

"You're Indian, Grant," he said, "you should be able tell by the sun."

I leaned back and studied him. He was serious. "Sorry there, Running Bull," I said.

"Well, yer Indian, ain't ya? Let's go."

We heard laughter and Herman's porch light turned on. We could hear them first, the laughter of women. First, I saw Meadow, who has three kids from three different men. As always, she walked ahead of everyone else—head down and quickly. *I know your father did something to you, Meadow*, I thought. I had been thinking of a way to ask her about it for years. The other women walked out of the porch towards us.

Clarence and I put the Halls behind our backs.

There were the twins: Susan "Little Steps" and Terri, who both still dance exactly the same way as they did when we were in high school. There was Lois in her beautiful Chevy-blue shawl, and there was Lona. Hell, even Karen was there. I didn't think Sam ever let her out of the house. And there was Rita, sexy Rita, grandmother at thirty-four— Rita who wrote *I love you* on the back of my hand in grade three.

Shit. There was my ex. As always, she still wouldn't look at me, and my face burned with all the pain still between us. I looked away but I caught her glance at me. She *almost* looked happy. Thank God we never had kids.

All of the women were laughing; some were even holding hands.

"It's eight o'clock, Clarence" I said.

"Eight bells? How'd you know that?"

I stood up. "Cuz I'm Indian."

There she was: Donna. She saw me and waved. She broke away from the group and they all called out, "Same time, next week!"

"Yeah, see yah!" she called back.

All the women started hooting and laughing, slapping their knees. They looked so happy. "Hayyy, Clarrennnce," they sang.

Clarence frowned and scratched his chin.

"Hello, gentlemen," Donna said and gave me a big hug. I could smell her long black hair and buried my nose in it. She smelled sooooooo gooooood.

"Donna," Clarence nodded.

"Grant!" Someone called. It was Herman.

"Howshegoin?" I waved. Donna slid her hand into my back pocket.

"Never better," he smiled. "You're on for Thursday—nine p.m.?"

"We'll be there."

I looked at Donna and held her by her waist. She smiled and blushed in my arms.

"Hey you. You're glowing."

"Hey you," she whispered and placed something in my right hand. I looked. It was a pack of yellow Halls. I smiled at her and winked. I kissed her and used my tongue to gently push my Halls into her mouth. Her eyes lit up and she smiled.

"Clarence," I said. "Thursday. Nine bells. Make sure your Indian ass is here. There's gonna be a talking circle for men and you're invited."

Clarence kicked the gravel behind us. Donna and I walked away.

"Take me home, baby." She nibbled my ear lobe, smiled, then burst into laughter.

Why Ravens Smile to Little Old Ladies
as They Walk By...

I wanted to record an erotic story I heard from the Dogrib Nation. I heard it one summer when I was working with kids on a fishing island in the middle of the Great Slave Lake, north of Yellowknife, NWT. This was before I met my wife, Pam, and before the death of our daughter, Isabell. The story is about how Raven acquired such a beautiful, flaming red tongue. When a Raven opens its beak towards you, look in. You will see a beautiful pink pussy in its mouth.

Really.

The story goes like this: A long time ago, the Dogrib people had kicked the shit out of Raven. They had it with the fucker. He had tricked, shamrocked and shananagined them one time too many. The Dogrib are magnificent fighters. Executing cowboy kicks, bannock slaps and aerial maneuvers, they are acrobats of destruction when they battle and I'm so proud to be one. Anyway, this wasn't the first time they kicked the shit out of Raven, but they sure wanted it to be their last. As Raven buckled, his face swollen, his left eye rammed shut, the people decided to rip off his beak. They did, too, the bastards. They pulled it right the hell off and ran back to town. With his black body ruined and crushed, Raven fell inside a coma.

How the Dogrib hid Raven's beak was they gave it to a blind, old woman. They told her what they had done and she agreed to hide it. She was a powerful medicine woman and they trusted her. She knew what to do. The old woman hid it under her dress, placing it between her thighs, pointing down. The long dress she wore prevented anyone from seeing the hard, black beak. With the beak, came Raven's tongue.

The tongue, lonely for a mouth, sought her sunshine spot, tasting and wiggling itself all the way in, as far as it would go. The old woman jumped when she first felt this, but soon loved what she felt.

It was delicious.

From that day on, the old woman experienced such intensity that she was dizzy and lost and wonderful all at the same time. Well, she just had to stay home. Why leave the house?

Thinking their mother was sick, her daughters would bring her food. The old woman insisted she was all right and smiled for the first time in years. All day she would bounce, bend over, wiggle and rock back and forth. The tongue loved its newfound mouth and this reborn woman loved her newfound, secret friend!

This went on for weeks. The old woman had never been happier.

Raven, however, was on the lookout for his beak and tongue. Because Raven's sense of taste was gone, the nose behind his beak had developed an excellent sense of smell. He walked into Fort Rae and demanded the Dogrib people return his beak at once. No one knew anything; that's what they told him. Raven said he wouldn't leave until he found his beak. He had grown skinny and people asked if he had a tapeworm. He told them all to fuck right off. He sat and glared, watching everyone in the community.

It wasn't long before he overheard the old woman's daughters talking about their mother. They were concerned that, being blind, their mother was no longer coming outside to visit. They were concerned that perhaps she was wanting to die. They said they had heard her moaning all hours of the night, sometimes crying out with a heavy voice.

"Perhaps," one said, "she is depressed."

"No, no," the other daughter said. "She's never looked happier."

The Raven senses tingled! Raven shot up and ran towards the old woman's house. He walked straight in and the old woman was on all fours, rocking herself and arching her back. She shot up and straightened out her dress, "Who is it?"

Raven changed his voice, "It is me, your daughter. I have come to do your laundry."

"I'll do it myself," she said. "Leave me alone."

"Are you sick, Mother?" the voice asked.

"No," she answered, "just tired."

Suddenly, Raven jumped the old woman and pulled her dress up. There was his beak between her thighs! He pulled but his tongue wouldn't let go. He pulled and pulled with all his might, and finally it came loose. He placed his beak snuggly back on and was about to walk out the door but stopped to drink what was in his mouth. "Holy lick!" he said.

Raven looked at the old woman and smiled. She winked and smiled back! She had strong medicine and could still feel his tongue inside her. Raven licked at the inside of his beak, enjoyed his new found friend, which was now secured in his mouth and flew back, beak intact, to the sky to plot more tricks on the Dogrib people.

And I know he was smiling all the way.

That is why, even to this day, when you see a raven open its mouth towards you, you will see a flaming red tongue and a beautiful pink pussy inside. And this, too, is why we ravens smile to little old ladies as they walk by.

Mahsi Cho!

the uranium leaking from port radium and rayrock mines is killing us

and the girl with sharp knees sits in her underwear. She is shivering.
The bus is cold. The man at the gun store has seagull eyes. Freckles
grow on the wrong side of his face. This town has the biggest
Canadian flag anywhere. It is always tangled and never waves. For
grass this playground has human hair. It never grows on Sundays. The
kids that play here are cold and wet. They are playing in their underwear. They are singing with cold tongues. They have only seven fingers
to hide with.

Those are rotting clouds. This is the other side of rain. The band plays
but there is no sound. I snap my finger but there is no sound.

There is someone running on the highway. There is no one in the field.
Nobody knows the cats here. No one knows their names.

They are letting the librarian's right eye fuse shut. There is a pencil stabbed
thru her bun. She can read "I didn't pop my balloon the grass did" in
my library book. She looks into me. One eye is pink. The other is blue.

My father said take the bus. There is yellow tape around my house. A
finger is caught in the engine but they only rev it harder. There are
cold hands against my back. I want to kiss Pocahontas before she dies
at age 21. Someone is stealing the dogs of this town while doctors
hold babies high in black bags. My mother's voice is a dull marble

rolling down her mouth, stolen to her lap, not even bouncing, not even once. She has sprayed metal into her hair. I am sitting on a red seat. My hands open with rawhide.

This is the ear I bled from. There is a child walking in the field. He is walking with a black gun.

In my girlfriend's fist is a promise. She does not raise herself to meet me. Her socks are always dirty. She is selling me a broken bed so she can lie on plywood. Her feet are always cold. The coffee we drink is cold. The bus driver does not wave goodbye. Why are there only children on this bus? Why are we wet and cold? Why are we only in our underwear?

I want to run but I have no legs. The tongue that slides from my mouth is blue.

Friday is the loneliest day of the week she says. The blanket she knitted this winter is torn upon us. She laughs at me with blue eyes. She says if you walk in the rain no one can tell you're crying. The soup we drink after is cold. The popcorn we eat after is cold. Someone is crying in the basement. Someone is crying next door.

The dream we have is something running on four legs, running on pavement towards us. It is running from the highway. It is a dead caribou running on dead legs. I meet its eyes but there are only antlers. In between the antlers is an eye. It too is cold and watching. Its eye is the color of blue.

The plants here have no flowers. The trees themselves are black. The fish are rolling sideways. Rain has started to fall.

The child with the black gun sees my house. He is walking backwards towards me. He swings his head. His eyes are blue. *Can you please sing with me?*

The bus driver does not wave goodbye.

The band is playing but all I hear is galloping.

I snap my finger.

My eyes are blue.

All I can hear is galloping…

The Night Charles Bukowski Died

Why did I play the water loud as Mikey cried in the shower well two nights ago we took him to the field and showed him how to punch kick defend himself and I think of the time we went for lunch at the caf and I said Ho Mikey yer sitting the wrong way you can't see the babes if you're facing the wall

Not he said I'm not facing the wall I'm looking out the window behind you

I turned and for the first time saw a mountain thrust clear through the clouds and for a moment I turned to Mikey who was smiling and took a picture with my heart and last night 2 am there was Scott

Fat red-head rugby playing Scott

180 pounds

Fat knuckled

Thick legged

Mean

Doggy on all fours muddy socks wet vomiting into the toilet and he and I were going to fight the night before cuz he was making fun of Mikey who's THIS close to killing himself and I said Don't be a fuck

Scott said What? Chill out God it was only a joke

And I was THIS close to burning him cuz Mikey can't defend himself He's 19 He's had two complete breakdowns so far He's on drugs for his screaming He said When I was a kid I just couldn't stop screaming I couldn't hold onto my emotions like other kids I was different

Scott puked on the floor in the dorm bathroom he said I'm not sorry about trying to get Mikey to eat that glue stick

I said You better lay off him

Fuck off he said The retard's here on a computer scholarship and forgets to wipe his ass He shouldn't be here and heaved some more I studied the back of his neck and thought if he were a rabbit I would take him with my teeth and there is sickness everywhere in this dorm nobody flushes you can smell it in the piss on my socks when I go back to my room and in my room we were playing dominoes when Scott stormed in and teased Hey Mikey why don't you finish eating this glue stick

I thought I should hurt him scoop his eye in or rip his nose away

And J was there he saw it all and after I kicked Scott outta my room the air hung heavy After Mikey left quiet Jason said Something has to be done I hate guys like that I hate white boys like that I hate them We gotta do something I hate it

Looks like the kid the dog and the old man got eaten Jason says and looks up at the ceiling

We listen to the crying and blubbering in the shower and shake our heads

Mikey's talking to himself again and I don't think he knows it So I'll have to move out at the end of the month cuz Scott heard my screaming and the shit is gonna fly when the dorm finds out what we did

Shit

And Mikey was THIS close to crying when he said They pennied my door shut and I didn't know who to call This was before I knew you I wish I knew you then

I asked How the hell does anyone penny your door shut

They slammed my door shut and three guys pushed it to the

frame while someone pushed pennies into the frame to lock the door closed I couldn't open it I knocked on the door for two hours and Scott was laughing in the hallway going You like that retard? You're on the third floor retard Why don't you jump? JUMP!

I wanted Mikey to take this take this roar in his head take a black shotgun and light this whole dorm up just grab Scott gut peel and skin him and go just go til he hits the province line and and Dominoes we showed Mikey how to play Dominoes for the first time in his life and when I picked up my seven they sounded like bones and Jason told us a baby caribou cries like a cat and I watch Mikey cover his smile with his small hands and I think of him this poor first year kid with eyes so close I get a headache if I look into them for too long falling in love with all his waitresses and I wonder what it'll be like for him the first time he goes down on the woman who takes him he with such beautiful little songs on the wind his eyes closed as he holds her hands his tongue parting lips and her going I can feel the sky diving between my legs don't stop oh please don't and the roar in his ears as she locks her thighs around him the same roar in his head when he was locked in his room for TWO HOURS Scott booming a basketball off the penny locked door going You like that Retard? You like that?

And Mikey can't hear a thing He can't hear a thing
For once
You listening Mikey? Jason asks These are fighting stories from home We're trying to make you strong and Mikey nods I tell him there was a moment there when a Slavey elder stood between his grandchild and a silver tipped grizzly and surrender was never a moment on anyone's lips He had an ax in his hand looking at a silver tipped grizzly with his grandson standing behind him No there was

nothing on his lips but COME THE FUCK ON LET'S DO THIS and Mikey
said Wow neat and Jason asked Did you understand the story Mikey?
Do you understand what we're trying to give you? And Mikey says I
think so

I think so

We nod good and pull balaclavas from under the mattress

Mikey doesn't hold out his hand so we hold it out for him and
squeeze I'm taping my knuckles and listening to the Cranes now and
man they know that Carnival means the celebration of spinning until
the meat flies from your body and I'm thinking the woman who takes
him stands THIS close to Mikey before it happens and she says You're
always laughing It's the most beautiful sound in the world and he will
put his scream away

You have no pupils she says

I do he goes

I have to stand THIS close to you to see them she says

And he can feel the break of her laughter against his face and
she tells him The reason the dogs bark at you when you walk down the
street is they know you ate a dog in another life and they can still
smell it on your breath and they go crazy biting their own tails and
each other's It's your scent not you they hate she says and rises to
kiss him and hold him and he closes his eyes and they fall to their
knees in secret

I hold my seven dominoes and say Mikey here's what we're
gonna do We're gonna wear these balaclavas and you and Me and
Jason are gonna get Scott and Mikey goes Wull are we gonna really
beat him up?

I go Yeah we'll roll him

And Mikey goes Yeah we'll roll him on the ground
And Jason and I laugh

I called home and told mom about Mikey and Scott and I had
to stop and open the windows and wipe my eyes and go Everybody in
this dorm knows he bullies Mikey but nobody does anything
Nobody
They're just as brutal to each other here as they are back
home Me and J are on the first floor we can't always watch him and I
drop my dominoes and pray Mikey'll drop Scott cuz tonight the dogs
back home jump in the air spin and try to snap their chains and Me
Mikey and J played Dominoes and CHARLES BUKOWSKI AT THE
SWEETWATER on disc and I was so disappointed when we finally heard
CB's voice and me and J agreed Bukowski should have had the voice of
a monster not a boy and Mikey asked who is Bukowski? And we said
you know Barfly? The movie? The poet? The guy who said he was *on
fire like the hands of an acrobat*
And Jason played his sacred pipe the one he saves for weeping
And tonight we waited in the black no moon shadows Me Mikey
and Jason in balaclavas on the proving ground and Scott staggered
from the direction of the campus bar carrying a six pack moving slow
I'm thinking he works out
wears a mean face
loves to ride a soul to pieces
has a girlfriend—
Why?
Mikey Jason whispers rolling his hood down There's your silver
tipped grizzly Let's tear the night to pieces

Mikey looks at him and I think for a second he's going to wave to Scott

I run

Jason blows his pipe and Scott stops *Who's there?*

J blows his pipe again and I let loose my war cry I remember for a second that there is a lion in Africa the hunters call He Who Greets With Fire

Mikey stands in the bushes and watches Scott who's tilted looking around I strike his throat throw him down while Jason boot staples Scott's nose to his face

Scott drops

moaning down

his fat hands trying to plug his gurgling I look at Mikey and yell Now's your chance! Mikey just stands there his balaclava not even down and J looks around and goes Come on man MOVE! But Mikey just stands there I can see his face and I think He's laughing at us He's fuckin' laughing at us I grit my teeth then it hits me he's crying standing there stupid fucking RETARDED—

HEY! Someone calls and we grab Mikey back into the campus forest and he falls and trips HEY! Someone calls again—CAMPUS SECURITY—STOP!!

We lay low as there are two of them They run past and Mikey is holding his hands to his face He's crying sobbing and I'm wet from the grass and Jason has point and motions We're okay

I whisper Mikey why didn't you do it? We were holding him man You could have busted him

And Mikey holds himself and cries You beat Scott up You hurt him I want to go home

I want to
go home I
want to go
home
I hold him this skinned caribou crying like a cat this little kid
who never stopped screaming As he cries into my chest Jason looks
down his bamboo flute broken I
throw
back
my
head
and
roar

Sky Burial

Pain seared up Icabus' leg forcing him to stop and wince. He wheezed through one lung, and the mall blurred around him. He coughed and his chest sounded and felt as if it were stuffed with the broken glass of gray light bulbs. This was it: he was dying. The Cree medicine had him.

In his reflection, Icabus hated what he saw. *I'm not that skinny, am I?* He was bleeding inside and felt so weak. "I seen better lookin' corpses." Something had blown behind his left eye earlier that morning, causing his ears to ring.

The bird. It was dying in front of him. He didn't know what the bird was called but was awed at how bright and blue the feathers were.

Parakeet? Parrot? No, he knew it wasn't the true name of the bird's tribe, and he wished he knew. He thought of all the shampoo bottles his daughter Augustine had and chose the one that smelled the best.

"Papaya," he said. "That's your Dogrib name now: Papaya."

The pet store, which showcased the bird, held it in a cage. The bird measured three feet from black beak to bright blue tail, yet the cage only offered four. A sign read: "Do Not Tap Cage." The bird was upside down, shitting on itself and biting at the chain that sliced into its leg.

The bird, he thought, *deserved something far better than this*.

Oh, how Icabus wished to be around fire. He was sure the bird was a woman. She panted; her black tongue licked at her swollen ankle. She hung awkwardly, rested, shivered, tried to bite at the chain, fell back, shivered again. It looked as if she were drowning. Icabus watched the bird and felt under his shirt where he was bleeding inside. It was if he had been force-fed thousands of porcupine quills that were growing with each breath. He pressed into his left rib cage as he strained to open the cage.

"Macaw," a voice said suddenly behind him.

"Huh?"

"It's a Macaw."

Icabus turned to look at the wielder of such a firm voice. It was a child. An Indian girl. Tall, slim. She was beautiful. Her eyes were large and round. She wore a T-shirt with a huge white owl with yellow eyes on it. A younger white boy with a runny nose came up and started banging on the cage. The girl left as fast as she had appeared. Icabus wanted to talk to her, but he was hit again with pain. He coughed and coughed and coughed. He held himself up against the glass and looked down until the reddest blood dripped from his mouth. He had to hurry, but where was the sign?

Icabus bought a coffee and a doughnut at Grandma Lee's. As he sat, the pain bit again as if the quills inside him were starting to burrow and grind inside his guts, shredding everything inside him. He put his head down and focused on his shoes. He took a breath, biting the tip of his tongue. *Chinaman did a good job on polishing them up*, he wiggled his toes. *Too bad the bitches got me.*

Any other man, he coughed, *any other man would not have woken up from last night's sleep*. Each heartbeat drove a long hot metal blade through his skull over and over. This was not the flu. It was a death sentence for what he and the boy had done to the sweat lodges in Rae.

Together he and Morris had burned them all. Icabus wanted to teach the Crees not to charge money for their sweat lodges on Dogrib soil, but the lesson had cost him everything—or had it? Was there still time? He'd thought last night about passing on his medicine to Morris, but Icabus had seen black around him before he left, and he knew Morris' days were numbered.

If he thought about it, he'd start to cry and if he started to cry here he'd never stop. The boy would have to look after himself. Their time was getting closer, and he knew it.

No more sunrises, no more northern lights, no more snow or cold or anything…and it had to be here, in a mall of strangers. All he could do was look down and think. His shoes were so polished they looked like black ice. In the reflection he watched the shadows and saw a man walking towards him. *Morris? My adopted son?*

"There you are," Harold said and sat beside him.

The pain struck again. Icabus bit into his doughnut. The dough would soak up the blood inside him. The noise of the mall rose around him: the metal-whine of blenders, children hollering for toys. Harold had a tray of Cokes and tacos and the smell was thick and sweet.

"We were looking for you. God, you look sick."

Icabus stared out the window to the mall parking lot. His ear began to ring again. A blonde child stood crying in the middle of the pavement, her red balloon flying away. One of her shoes was off. Behind her, the Edmonton sunset tore the sky in half. Icabus squinted but couldn't see a parent for the girl. He leaned forward, tracking the balloon as far as he could. He wanted so desperately to follow it.

"I see you got your shoes fixed." Harold took the paper bag and looked inside. "What else?"

Icabus glared at him for not asking first. "Safes," he grumbled. "Suzy Muktuck's in town." He studied Harold's throat and hated how white it was.

"Icabus," Harold blushed. "Nobody calls them safes anymore. Did Augy say you could afford these?"

Icabus ignored the question and wiped cold sweat from his forehead. *I'm dying. They got me bleeding to death inside.*

"I don't understand why you got those fixed up," Harold scoffed. "You don't even have enough money for next week. Christ, you've been eating at our place the last four days..."

"Gotta look good at my funeral, " Icabus explained.

Harold missed it. "If I hear another trapping story, I don't know what I'll do."

"Our family comes from the land. You need to remember this."

Harold rolled his eyes and bit into the taco. Tomato sauce gushed out the bottom. Icabus closed his eyes. The sauce was blood. Augustine's blood every time she tried to have a baby, the blood of his son who had killed himself, the blood in his piss and spit.

Harold went on talking with a full mouth. Icabus nodded, pretending to pay attention. He sipped his coffee and waited for a sign. "Where's Augy?" He asked.

"Looking for you." Harold bit into the taco again and Icabus looked for the little girl. She was gone.

"There you are," an exhausted voice heaved. Augustine huffed towards them: her bad perm, pink track pants, Jean jacket, dusty runners. She sat down, grabbed the other taco, and elbowed Harold. "And you!" she scolded, "this is cold." She bit into it anyway. Icabus studied his daughter and her husband. He looked into her dreadful perm and thought, *Spider legs, thousands of spider legs.*

The couple gabbed. Food toppled out of their mouths. Their noise was muffled and lost to the crowd.

It will be okay, he thought. He'd left his wedding band by his bed. The day before, when Harold had assumed he was at the dentist's, he'd emptied his account and left his money in his wallet under his pillow. Three thousand dollars in thirty 100 dollar bills would go far for them. As for his clothes, they would all be burned once he left. Icabus looked around.

To his right, a table away, sat a family of ruined Indians. They had all let themselves go. They fed on burgers, fries, shakes. The mother had cut her hair. The kids were pudgy. The man was soft. Where are the warriors? Icabus had been waiting for a nod or a sign of acknowledgment, but the Indians wouldn't meet his eyes. *What's happened to us?* he thought. *What the hell has happened to all of us?*

"Oh," a breath lit from his mouth. It was the young girl he saw, the one with the owl shirt. Augy and Harold kept talking, taking turns sucking the straw, biting into more tacos.

Her long black hair was what caught him. She was as slender as a diamond willow. She moved with a white woman across the perimeter. What the hell was she doing with a white woman? They carried hot dogs and drinks. The girl sat down quickly out of his view. He shifted to see her better.

"...and the lady, Dad. The lady said we could visit Sundays and we could bring you home cooked food. It'll be good for you to be with others your own age." Augy ate while Harold listened and nodded. "You'll love it."

"The move will be good for you." Harold added. "Think of all the French Safes you could use over there."

Icabus nodded again and looked for the young girl. A young couple was in his way. They had their lower lips pierced and whenever they kissed Icabus could hear metal clicking, clicking. *Savages*, he thought. He squinted and saw her. She was nodding, listening to the white woman speak.

Icabus sat straight up and almost spilled his drink. He brought his hand up over his lip and caressed the whiskers on his chin. *She's the one*, he thought. It was her shirt that did it. The white owl was the sign he'd been looking for.

"I'm Stan the man with the nine!" Stan would yell to the women who drank with them. "When I die, there's gonna be two boxes: one for Stan and one for the nine!" The women would giggle and Stan would always throw Icabus a wink.

It was the winter of '79. They were drinking at Stan's. Icabus was taking a leak outside a party when he looked up and saw a huge white owl looking down at him. What he remembered most was the eyes. Yellow eyes. With fire and power behind them. They were eyes he couldn't lie to. Eyes he couldn't tame. The eyes saw him for what he really was: a drunk.

The owl hissed at him as he ran back to his shack. He grabbed his .410 and Stan ran after him.

"Lookit' this fuckin' owl!" Icabus hooted. "Look!"

They were both drunk and Stan made the sign of the cross when he saw the owl.

Stan yelled, "Someone's gonna die! Don't shoot it!" but Icabus aimed and fired. "I didn't mean to hit it," he would say later, but they saw an explosion of white feathers. Stan punched him hard, catching his ear. Icabus fell down. Stan ran into the snow to help the bird. It was dead.

Neither of them buried the bird, and Icabus never spoke to Stan ever again.

The next time Icabus saw the owl, it was in a dream. He dreamt he was walking in the snow to the old trapline he and Stan shared as kids when the owl landed in front of him. The eyes of the owl had changed. They were Stan's.

Icabus woke as Augy ran into his room saying that Stan had died. Family had called from Rae. A stroke had taken Stan during the night.

The pain hit again. Icabus bit his cheek so he wouldn't scream. "It's gettin' closer," he whispered. He thought of his wife who had died far too young from the cancer. Delphine. He thought of her grace, her elegance. The community thought she was so shy, but Icabus knew that she saved the very best of herself for him. Oh, they had argued; they had yelled, but the passion and the peace between them grew every year they had together. He missed her love and was sad at the loss she left behind. *God took you*, he thought, *and I never got to hear everything you had to say.*

After her funeral, whenever he saw a butterfly, he would call her name. And whenever he saw a red fox, he would whisper his son's name and weep with guilt because his son died alone and ashamed. *It will be something*, he thought, *to see you both again: young, alive and radiant.* In his dreams, Icabus walked into the Great Slave Lake by his home in Rae as he died, releasing himself to it, and disappearing.

On CBC, before he left Rae, the Dogrib leaders were telling everybody to boil the water twice before drinking it. They never said why.

He shook his head. *We can't drink it, but we bathe in it.* He took a long breath. Using the table, he pulled himself up slowly and stood still as the blood roared in his ears. He could taste blood in his saliva.

"Where are you goin'?" Harold asked.

"To sing for the last time," Icabus answered.

43

"What?"

Icabus began to sing under his breath. He walked carefully, cautiously. His lips moved and he felt the wind gather around him. He walked slowly in his polished shoes, almost as if making a deal with the pain to give him just a little more time, just a little more, and there she was. She and the white woman were eating their hot dogs. The girl was the first to see him. "Mommy," she said. "Look at the Indian."

The mother gawked towards him and warned, "Now, honey..."

"Scuse me," Icabus said, all the while hoping he'd have enough time. The mother looked around, perhaps for Security, but the girl watched him. "There's something in your daughter's hair."

"What!" the mother squawked. "Where?" She went through her daughter's hair. "Oh, Mindy..."

Mindy wouldn't stop looking at him.

Icabus tried to smile through all of the pain inside of him. "I'm a Dogrib Indian. Have you ever heard of us?"

The mother stopped briefly looking through Mindy's hair and watched him. "Please have a seat. My daughter is Cree."

He held his back, leaned into the table, careful of his knees, and sat slowly across from them. He winced and bit his lip. "It's okay if you haven't."

"But your hair is short," Mindy said.

Icabus laughed, surprised with the observation. "Our hair is short. We're different that way from the Crees, but we pray the same."

Icabus began singing inside and could feel the power rising around him. He ran his fingers through his hair and pulled three hairs from his scalp. From the inside of his jacket, he pulled out his gift for the girl.

"Well," Mindy's mother exhaled, "I can't find anything."

"It's right here." Icabus explained. He leaned forward, passing the gift from one hand to the other, before feeling through Mindy's hair. He felt the waves of a hot lake, the down on a duck's belly, the underflesh of a thousand petals.

"Can I give you something?" he asked.

She smiled and nodded.

"Look!" he said and brought back a bright blue feather. He pulled a few hairs from her head when he pulled back the feather.

"Oh my," the mother grinned. "Oh my!"

"Oh, Mommy," Mindy clapped, "it's beautiful!"

"For you." Icabus offered it to Mindy. "From the bird."

"The Macaw!" Mindy beamed.

"When a woman gives birth to a girl," he offered, "the girl is the father's teacher."

Under the table, he wrapped her hair around his fingers.

"I'm my daddy's teacher?" Mindy asked.

"You're the one," he finished. *Yes, he would teach her.* He sang. He called it forth and it came. The young girl giggled and covered her mouth. A hand grabbed onto Icabus' shoulder almost breaking the song.

"Here he is!" Harold called. "Over here, Augy!"

Icabus looked down.

"Dye aye kae khlee nee," he whispered and looked over to Mindy. "Remember me."

"Can I keep the feather?" she asked.

He coughed and nodded. "Do you like cats?"

Mindy shook her head. "I'm allergic."

"You can't use your medicine around cats," he said. "They'll steal it."

"What do you mean?" the mother asked.

"In your life, you need to listen with the deepest part of you for what to do. You need to listen with your blood."

"That is good advice," the mother pulled out her purse. "What tribe are you from again?"

"Dogrib," he answered and when he spoke, he smiled. This was it. The mother wrote this down. "Is that one word or two?"

"Thank you," Mindy smiled and held the feather up to the light. Icabus was pleased.

"Dad!" Augy said and came over. "I'm so sorry," she apologized to the woman. "My father wanders." She cleared her throat and lowered her voice. "He's...confused."

Icabus sang louder now and began moving his lips. Maybe the girl would one day visit Rae with questions about him, questions that were asked by her blood and his medicine.

Icabus felt the song push against the back of his teeth and run its fingers through her hair. He thought of the lake and looked into Mindy's eyes. He sent part of himself: the best part. Mindy's eyes registered his power. She wasn't scared and that was good.

He sang and twisted her hair with his under the table. He remembered the song as best he could. It was the same song his grandmother had sung to him. He looked down to make sure his shadow covered Mindy's. The pain sliced again. He sang her name with a breath and all she heard was: "Deeeee..."

He pulled the braid of their hair until it snapped, and Icabus left his body. It was like falling skyward. Mindy received him: the

Macaw's blue feather in her hand; her mother pulling Mindy close; Augy, her bad perm blocking out the sun.

"Dad? Dad!"

Icabus flew with an explosion of white feathers and was swallowed by the hottest lake. He could hear the most beautiful songs being sung by thousands of voices, and there was peace. He became it. Everything was so blue, and he noticed that the colors red and black were nowhere to be seen. He could see Delphine waiting for him. She was radiant, standing in her tanned moosehide dress, and beside her stood Justin, who stood so proud. Morris wasn't here, and that was a good sign. Icabus looked to his left. Stan walked beside him, smiled, and placed his hand on Icabus' shoulder, guiding him home...

Snow White Nothing For Miles

Icabus once said there were 68 turns in the road from Yellowknife to Rae. Every time Morris took this road, he tried to keep count. What was he at now—37?

"Oh my woman don't love me my woman don't love me," Morris droned as he hunched forward on crackly Cheezie bags. He gunned the accelerator and the truck engine roared. "I'm a fuckin' cop a fuckin' cop and I can't get it up oh I can't get it up."

"Stupid!" He screamed. "How God damn stupid!"

Oh the rage—how he wanted to open the truck door, jump with his hands in the air, roll on the cold and blowing ground and scream face first into the snow as the truck rolled sideways, a rooster tail of sparks pluming the air. Maybe the snow in all her lush blanket wisdom could snap his back straight and pull the rage from his throat and all the nights spent in paralyzing fear and give him a hard-on an 18-year-old would be proud of.

38

"Have some time off," the Sarge had said, his beefy hand like a fat hindquarter on Morris' shoulder.

Have some time off—for what? Morris stopped himself. What do I have and what do I have left?

He had been driving for the past hour. The snow on the road was bright where the headlights bathed it and tonight was cold, so cold he could feel it in his marrow. He turned up the heater.

Morris could smell the bucket of cold Kentucky Fried Chicken on the floor. It disgusted him now. He rolled his side window down a pinch for fresh air. His right hand took the wheel while he held his palm there against the window. His flesh burned through. Like a brand.

40

He thought of that song he had heard on the radio that Malcolm and Henry kept playing in their "Hour of Power" out of Yellowknife. The song went:

"Kill the lights in the middle of the road and take a look around."

Morris was tempted to flick the lights off, slam on the brakes, seize the engine and scrape his body through the windshield, the glass teeth vomiting his sliced body onto the hood, ripping his cheek through the beak of the eagle head ornament carved out of caribou antler.

He wanted to call out to the sky, "Where were you when I needed you? Where?"

Icabus gave that carving to him. It was a present from his brother, Paul.

41

"Here I am", Morris thought, "racing from Yellowknife to Edzo, racing with building supplies for his home."

(Hey Hey! Whatcha Doin'?)

(Hey Hey!)

He remembered his rat-faced brother-in-law, Richard, not five inches from his face, yellow teeth, a plug of Red Man chewing tobacco pucked under his lower lip, eyes slit, a black cactus of Fu Man Chu whiskers sprouting from his chin.

"Hey Hey! Whatcha Doin'?!"

When he pulled up at the gas station in Rae, between Edzo

and Yellowknife, Richard with his rat-teeth ran up to his truck and threw back the tarp like some crazed husband throwing the blankets back on adulterous lovers. This exposed Tyvek paper, doors, screws, hammers, nails, and fresh groceries for a week.

"What the fuck is this?" he yelled. "How come you don't support local business, huh?"

These were all supplies for his house—all bought in Yellowknife at astounding savings with competitive prices, while Richard, that weasel fuck brother-in-law, owned both the grocery and hardware store in Rae and was ripping off every Dogrib in Rae and Edzo.

Fuck legislation. Morris wanted to give Richard the cobra claw and the pepper spray. He wanted to burn Richard's eyes shut, choke him out and drag him through the parking lot, screaming, "Nighty night, bastard!"

"Because I can't afford your prices," Morris said and finished pumping his gas.

And here he was again with new building supplies and fresh groceries, making a midnight run from Yellowknife to Rae. Morris eyed his stash of lights, touch-up paint and sealant in the cab. All for him and his house his house his house!

But Sheila—was she always this miserable? There was no end to the conspiracy! It was she who had squealed about his expeditions to Yellowknife to her brother, and it was she who squealed on him that he was buying bulk in Yellowknife, and it was she who sat in the truck while Richard ran to Morris' truck, peeled back the orange tarp and hollered, "HEY HEY! WHATCHA DOIN'?" in his face.

42

Fuck the benefits! Fuck the Red Serge!

"Go ahead, Rick ya prick!" he wanted to scream. "You load them up in your forty thousand dollar truck. You take it all back and demand a full fuckin' cash refund. You can do it all...just give me back my life!"

Morris checked the rear view mirror. The tarp was still tied down, covering his new push broom sticking out of the tarp, its smooth handle shivering against the wind.

43

(Hey Hey! Whatcha Doin'?)

Sheila stayed at Richard's now, *probably nagging the hell out of him to see why my truck wasn't in Rae or Edzo today.*

"Cuz I was in Yellowknife buying supplies and grub, ya dizzy shits!" He looked around like a punched puppy: eyes wide. "Hoo!" he yelled again. "Hey-ya!"

The force, Morris thought. They asked for nine chin-ups at the physical. I gave 'em forty! I didn't mind twelve-hour shifts on Christmas. I didn't mind twelve-hour shifts on New Years!

"Go home, Morris," the Sarge had said. "Take some time to...."

To what, go home to my family? What family?

"Go home. You look like shit."

The sign for Stagg River flashed by.

And this road of 67 turns—this road that was smoother in the winter than the summer thanks to the DPW Caterpillars. Yet how many Dogrib, Chip, Cree, Slavey, men, women, elders, and expecting mothers had died on this road?

"Brucey," his uncle whispered to his father. "When you hit

that road from Rae to Yellowknife, you go as fast as you can. Pedal to the metal. And don't stop for nothing. Lots of people died on that road. That's where the hitchhikers wait. Spirit boys with split hooves. You slow down. They'll hop on your truck and wait.

"When you get home, they'll hop on that caribou hindquarter or your luggage and you'll take them into your house. They will bring hell to you and your family. Never look in the rearview mirror cuz something might be lookin' right back."

"You can damn well bet," the Sarge once said taking a long slow drag, "that if those bureaucrats in Y.K. lived in Rae and had to commute their government asses to Yellowknife, they'd have that fucker paved in no time flat."

Icabus once whispered that he drove around the corner on the 41st turn and two boys were burning in their truck on that road. He could see their hands grabbing through the flames like the black wings of scared birds throwing themselves against the glass. Throwing themselves against a burning window. And the way it was going up, all he could do was watch. And the screaming, he said, woke him up every day.

That was on the 41st turn.

41

Old man Icabus. Where was he? That long-assed battle-axe burning everything down. Where was he?

After four years of criminology, after six months at Regina, after getting his bronze medallion and his silver cross, after getting all these "White man's carrots" as Icabus called them, Morris returned to Rae, his mother's soil, to learn more about the Dogribs and learn the language and culture.

He had gone for a coffee before meeting the Sarge. Two Dogrib boys sat at the table next to him.

"Do you smell bacon?" one asked, pushing his Dene Nation cap backwards.

"Yeah," the other answered. "Hickory-smoked and honey-glazed."

"Just as I thought," the first sniffed. "I smell pig."

The coffee shop roared with laughter as Morris looked out the window and tried not to blush.

"Whootsum mom?" a voice had asked from the table over.

An elder: Icabus. Sipping coffee out of a Styrofoam cup. "I'll say it in English. Who. is. your. mom?"

"Nishi," Morris answered. "Rosa Nishi."

"Named after old Fort Rae, the island," Icabus nodded. "Been there?"

Morris shook his head.

"Are you a honkey, or what?"

"Half," Morris answered. "I'm Metis."

"Piss on the Metis!" he said. "You're Tlicho—Dogrib."

Morris nodded. He felt naked. He still had his pig shave from Regina.

"Do you even know what a Dogrib looks like?" Icabus asked.

"I'm looking at one, aren't I?" he responded.

"Can you speak Dogrib?"

"Not yet," Morris answered. "I was raised in Smith."

"With the Chips and the Crees," Icabus nodded. "How old are you?"

"*This was a mistake*," Morris thought. He wanted to leave. "27."

"27? Christ, you're still shitting yellow, I guess!"

Toothless mouths exploded with laughter as elders, perched in the corner, slapped their knees and pointed.

That night the community threw a drum dance for Morris, welcoming him home as a Dogrib officer who had come home to help his people. They gave him a moose-hide jacket with glittering, thick beaded flower designs so pretty and so bright he blushed when the council of elders presented it to him.

Then the tea dance, where everyone held hands and danced in a circle. Fourteen Dogrib drummers bellowed prayer songs, power songs, thunder songs that lightened everyone's feet and hearts. The whole community danced in one circle. They called Morris in and he wore his jacket proudly, stood straighter and held his head high. When he came into the circle, he held hands with Icabus who took it strongly at first, but the cement floor stole Morris' energy. His legs felt rubbery, like he was dancing on shifting sand. He tripped on Icabus' feet causing smiles from people watching. Icabus slithered his hand away and pushed him.

"Metis!" he spat. "Your belly button's still wet! You don't know nothing! Get away from me." Icabus stomped off to the canteen leaving him with a burning face. But he danced. Morris danced. An elder, Melanie Wah-shee, showed him how. She showed him to step on the balls of his feet, to shift his weight and keep his rhythm. He spun, felt cocky, good. He looked up. Everyone was sweating, especially he, in his fresh Moosehide jacket. Melanie danced beside him, so beautiful, so patient. The truth was, Morris had always prayed he'd meet a Dogrib woman who'd take him as her husband and teach him the ways of his people. Sheila was supposed to be the answer to that prayer, but things had soured so quickly between them.

Coming home to the heart of Dogrib territory was a dream come true for him and he was so ready to learn anything anyone could teach him. He didn't care that Icabus was scowling at him. Melanie squeezed his hand and danced behind him, beside him, around him. He was Dogrib and so proud to be in the circle.

Morris gunned the accelerator and remembered the moose hide jacket. Where was it? When he wore it to supervise the kids playing volleyball at the Sportsplex, he wore it with pride. Old Icabus was there too, sipping tea, waiting until the kids had all left. Morris was rolling up the net, about to carry it in the storage room when strong hands slapped his shoulders and spun him around.

"Take it off!" Icabus demanded. "You didn't kill that moose for its hide. You're not a hunter."

"Wha— " Morris tried to ask with both surprise and shock.

"You give that jacket to me and I'll decide when you can wear it." Icabus growled.

Morris obeyed. He didn't know what Icabus had over him but he gave him his jacket and had to run home through a 30 below night with wind so cold he almost froze his nose and ears.

Whatever happened to that jacket? he thought.

42

A KFC box and a two beer cans flashed by in the ditch.

Then the sweat lodges came and everything, just everything changed.

He remembered the poster at first: "SWEAT LODGE" and the dates. There were two planned in one week: one for the women, one for the men. The three Cree women who ran the sweats held a meeting with the chief and band council saying that everyone was invited—for a price.

"Fifty bucks a head," the Sergeant grinned over coffee.

Icabus was waiting for Morris at his house after getting off work.

Morris swore he locked his door.

Icabus had let himself in and was sitting at the coffee table, legs crossed like a woman, moccasins on, jacket on, cap on, grim.

Hey, Gramps! he wanted to say, *Give us a smile, Grump!*

But Icabus was as cold and mean as war. "Sit down," he ordered.

"Well, can I have some coffee?" Morris asked.

"It's your house. Help yourself." Icabus said, as though Morris was the visitor. "Where's all your Indian tea?"

Morris issued the meanest look he could. "I'm all out."

The power he had over me, oh the power.

Icabus stared through him. "We have to do something."

"Oh yeah?" Morris responded, trying to maintain a firm voice like they taught at the academy. He puffed his chest out and tried to walk like the Sarge: a rolling tank, ready.

"I have to burn those sweat lodges down," Icabus said, "and I need your help."

What is it with Dogrib and fire? Morris wanted to ask. He looked down at the Kentucky Fried bucket at his feet. "What is it with the Dogrib and KFC?" Morris asked and laughed.

43

"Whoa — hold it right there," Morris wanted to say. "As an officer of the law...".

Icabus raised his hand and silenced him. "Be ready tonight," Icabus said, "around two."

Morris struggled, "I— "

Icabus put his cup down. "See you then." He stood up, paused before the porch, and slipped his moccasins into his black rubbers.

Morris sat incredibly still after Icabus left and he was met with a warm calm.

And I need your help.

Morris stood outside of Icabus' house not knowing what to do. His watch read two a.m. A chained husky with a dead ear sniffed the air towards him. It had the black mask of a bandit. Icabus opened his door. With him he carried a huge teddy bear. It was brown, fuzzy, smiling. *Was that where Icabus hid his medicine—in the belly of the bear?* There was a silence as the two men gauged each other.

"My ulcer's acting up," Icabus said. "You're ready?"

Morris nodded, trying not to laugh. Icabus almost looked human standing with that teddy bear.

"We'll take my truck. It's at my daughter's."

The dog eyed them both and wagged her tail. They walked along Fort Rae's HAP Houses. Morris noted the abundance of Ski-doos under tarps, waiting for winter and a smooth iced passage across the

Great Slave Lake. There were kids outside, playing in the dust, unattended. No wonder the elders were demanding a community curfew.

"Pah," Icabus spat, eyeing a house they passed. "That boiled owl."

"What?" Morris asked. He could see the window Icabus scorned. A curtain dropped back in place.

"Maggie. She'll be on the phone now telling everyone I'm walking with you."

"What's so bad about that?"

"They'll think I'm turning nark."

Morris laughed. It was funny how Icabus thought ten steps ahead.

"I don't know why you're laughing. Your tires will be slashed tomorrow from this gossip."

"Icabus is wise," Morris said to the sky. He was scared that people cruising by would remember them. If they did burn the sweat lodges down, the people would remember them walking together, especially Icabus and that ridiculous teddy bear.

"Do you know how they took out the last police officer who came to Rae?"

Morris stopped. "How?"

"Dry meat."

"Dry meat?" Morris challenged.

Icabus slowed down and covered his eyes. "Last officer that was here cleaned the town up good. Too good. Some people got together, made dry meat, gave it to the officer. Wade was his name."

Morris took a mental note, planning to verify it later with the Sergeant.

"They spit TB into the meat."

Morris stopped. "What?"

"They dried the meat in their house, played cards. All their cigarette smoke flew into the meat. When meat's wet, it's sticky. The smoke stuck to the meat. They found old Isadore with his TB. When he drinks he forgets to take his pills. They paid Isadore to put his bloody spit onto the meat. All his sickness went straight into the dry meat. The officer ate it. He got very, very sick. How many bags have you received since arriving?"

Morris' stomach rolled. "Three."

"Do you trust who made it?"

Melanie gave him one. She smoked hers outside. The other two—how the hell did he get the other two?

Two kids approached on ten speeds. "Do you smell dog shit?" a voice called out. It was the two boys from the coffee shop. They sped by. "Hickory-smoked and honey-glazed," the other with the Dene Nation cap answered. "I smell pig."

They laughed before Icabus spun around and yelled, "He's your cousin!"

Both boys stopped pedaling and sailed by. Their eyes were huge.

"There's my truck," Icabus said. "You'll drive."

"WORLD'S GREATEST JIGGER" is what the license plate said. Morris had to bite his tongue hard not to laugh again. He drove the old pick-up slowly over the bumps while Icabus used the huge teddy bear to pad his tummy from the seat belt. If anyone saw him driving, it would appear that he was the only one driving, him and that huge smiling brown bear. Morris shook his head. *Where did he get the other two bags of dry meat?*

The smoke from Saskatchewan fires had blown north, causing the sunset to ignite like a magnesium flare. The moon, bright and still, looked like a burning dime.

"You didn't lock your door." Morris said. There had been break-ins every day of the week this month.

"My brother, Paul, would dream it first before any Dogrib broke into our house."

"What if they were white?"

"Bingo has strong legs. She can break her chain if she has to. We'll walk from here."

Icabus, without his teddy bear, said nothing as they walked the highway to the campground.

Morris was surprised Icabus kept pace with him but he remembered always seeing Icabus walking the road from Edzo to Rae. He had heard from children that Icabus held council with nagha, the bushmen. It was rumored that he alone mediated between the Dogrib and the nagha in matters concerning the land and medicine. Could Icabus speak their language? Morris wanted to reach out and touch Icabus to make sure he was real.

"A very long time ago when my hair was black," Icabus started, "I was up in Deline. You been there?"

Morris looked over his shoulder. "No."

Icabus used a soft voice. Morris was surprised that this was the same man who could be so fierce. He was also surprised that

Icabus never moved his mouth when he talked. He could see the pulse of the carotid and the vocal mechanisms at work, but Icabus's lips never moved. "The Dene had a prophet, Ayah. Lots of inkwo."

"Inkwo?" Morris asked.

"He gave us rules, kind of like that little book you pull out of your pocket every time you're in court or charging Suzi Smoke for bootlegging."

"Anyways..." Morris egged him on.

"Anyways, Metis," Icabus smiled, "he warned us about sweat lodges. He called them big beaver lodges where the two-legged were allowed to rest. He said to watch out for them, that they did not belong to us. He said they were for the other Indians down south and that we have our own ceremonies. These were in the days when you thought a blow job was a long kiss on a windy day."

Morris laughed, surprised with Icabus' humor. As they walked past the dump, Morris held his breath. He could smell the rot and grunge of black garbage smoldering. On the wire fence that lined the dump, children had tied slaughtered seagulls so they looked like the birds were flying, or sitting, or diving upside down. Twenty birds at least. The only thing that gave their death away was their limp necks.

"Spooky," Morris thought.

Icabus stared. Black caterpillars of burnt plastic twirled in the air, falling everywhere. Morris watched the plastic land on his pullover and in his hair. The night smelled raw. Icabus sneezed and held his tummy.

"Where are we going?" Morris asked.

"Camp grounds," Icabus said.

"How do you know the sweats are here?"

"Here these Indians braid their hair and dress in long skirts: no watches, no gold; yet they stay at Arnie's, the most expensive place in town."

"How much?"

"Over one hundred and twenty a night."

Morris shook his head. They walked and the sun bit the horizon, causing the sky to bleed dusk. "Do you think," he asked, "that maybe the Dogrib should adapt and take sweat lodges in?"

"Cree medicine isn't ours, and not when money's involved."

"They gotta pay their bills."

Icabus stopped on the road and pushed Morris. "It's not our way," Icabus said. "The Dogribs who have medicine are starting to ask for money as payment. The day you start involving white man's money for Indian medicine, it dies."

The push hadn't been hard; it was more of a scold than anything. Morris was about to turn around and confront Icabus about his bullying when Icabus walked passed him and started to talk.

"One of my girls lives in Edmonton," he continued, as if nothing had happened, "going to school to be a counselor. She said one time she was at a conference for women, with a bunch of other Dogribs. The people who made this meeting were holding sweats. My girl started to feel funny when she saw them set up and she couldn't sleep at night. When asked if she was going to go in, she said no. My girl said she was on her time, and they asked her if she could watch the fire outside, keep the rocks hot. She said okay."

"When those Dogrib women went in, my girl wanted to tell them to stop. She said it was like a bad dream. It looked like they were being swallowed. She said it was quiet at first but then you could hear singing and praying. She watched the fire. Then, not even fifteen minutes into it, a Dogrib woman came out vomiting. She was cold to the touch, just like she had died, my girl said. Then another and another. They all came out vomiting. Some were crying. Others stayed sick for two days after. My girl said the organizers asked them not to tell anyone and insisted it must have been the food they had eaten. I don't think so."

The campground was just around the corner. Morris felt exhilaration in hearing these stories.

"It's not our way," Icabus continued. "When I was a kid, I watched something like a sweat lodge. One of my cousins was sick, so sick he could hardly move. My father dug a hole in the ground where the man could lay and he made a stove out of clay. He put water in the stove and dropped red rocks into the water. Steam surrounded the man and went inside of him. They covered the man with caribou hides over red willows. The man's sickness came out in his sweat. We did this for two days. We prayed, gave offerings to the fire."

"That was when I learned to pray to the moon at night and pray to the sun during the day and to always pray to fire when you see it. That is our way."

"So now," Morris offered, "you and I are going to burn something that might help many people?"

"We have a direct link with the Creator. We don't have to pay fifty bucks so he'll listen," Icabus answered. "It all comes from inside. You watch a candle, it dies from the inside. People are like that too. They leave it to the white man and his pills, rather than search out for themselves what's killing them. They're too eager to trust someone else's medicine."

They were quiet. Morris thought back to the phone call he had made earlier that day.

"Sarge, tell me about Icabus."

The Sarge blew, like someone stole his breath. "Why?"

"Just noticed him around town, that's all. Wanna know the scoop."

"Best I can figure," the Sarge said, "that man's someone who could have turned the Dogribs around. Powerful, just powerful...used to drink! Boy, he'd be in the tank every night. We didn't have to mop the place for a month. He did it for us. But one morning, I was about two hours late, and I had a feeling Pete fell asleep again guarding. So I come in and I peeked around the corner and, sure enough, Pete's little head was between his little hands. So I pulled the fire alarm and he pissed his pants hopping around! I didn't know whether to laugh or holler at him."

"'What if Icabus would have choked on his puke or slipped into a coma?' I yelled. 'He's got the diabetes, ya know!' Or he used to. I dunno if he cured hisself or what, but anyways, I went to let him go and air the place out but he was gone. That little Dene was gone! I grabbed Pete and hollered, 'What the hell did you do with Icabus?'"

"Pete told me he had been sleeping for only an hour and I checked the log book. It was true. Icabus was recorded as snoring away, laying in his own piss. But he was gone, Morris. He'd escaped."

"So I took the car, went to his house, knocked on his door and let myself in. The old guy was having coffee. He was shaved, showered, was wearing fresh clothes, and he had that cocky little smile on his face.

"'You're late,' was all he said. Cock-knocker!"

"'How the hell did you get out of the tank?' I asked. 'Did you give Pete a lickin', or what?'"

"'Have some coffee, 'he told me. Here he made a jailbreak and was offering me coffee. You're damn rights I had a coffee—and a smoke!"

"'Icabus,' I asked, 'goddamn you, man! How the hell did you get out of the tank!?'"

"'Keyhole,' he said."

"Keyhole! Well, we just sat there with my hair standing straight up and a squirt of piss in my shorts!"

"He told me he turned to smoke," the Sarge had told him, "and I believe him."

Goose bumps rolled across Morris' arms. "You said he used to drink. Why'd he stop?"

"He killed his boy."

"What?"

"His son, Justin, was gay, and one day he told his dad. Icabus covered his eyes and said, 'My only son is dead today. He died. I am alone in the world now. I'll never speak his name again.' Well, Justin hung himself in the city."

43

Morris remembered watching the orange flames storm and dance in the reflection of Icabus' eyes.

"It starts tonight," Icabus said.

They had gotten to know one another, he and Icabus. But then things started to change. Icabus was suspected of shooting someone.

What it boiled down to was Rick Weza, an out of work carver, was drinking and hunting. He saw an eagle; he shot the eagle. When he returned to Rae, he had an eagle's dismembered head and two claws stuffed in a black garbage bag. Feathers and feet sold down south in a black market and he had contacts in Yellowknife. An eagle feather could fetch hundreds of American dollars from rich New Agers. Even powwow dancers from other tribes who needed a feather from the north to complete their regalia were willing to trade trucks, rifles, money—all for a single feather.

When Rick walked to the café for coffee the next day, he was shot through both hands by a .22. Even though Rick could never carve again, charges were never pressed. It was never brought up in the detachment and the Sarge told Morris to let it die down. It did. Morris heard maybe it was Rick Weza who sicked medicine on Icabus.

Maybe.

But Morris remembered the dream. He and Icabus were spending time together checking nets and camping out on the fishing islands on Great Slave Lake. Morris enjoyed sitting on pamper moss and spruce bows in the smokehouse with Icabus eating fresh dry fish. Icabus was a superb cook, often sprinkling blueberries into his bannock dough. Morris relaxed with the good eating and sipped tea. But after a late night of storytelling and listening to the lake water lap against the island rock, Morris dreamed something horrible.

Icabus was standing frozen in a room where his daughters played cards. Morris was in the room too, watching, waiting. Something was about to happen. He could feel it. He was watching Icabus try to break up the card game. It was late. Morris, in the dream, suddenly realized he was talking with Icabus' daughter, Connie. He was making progress. They were sharing a laugh and she was teasing him about his gun. She wanted to hold it and Morris was shaking his head, smiling. She kept reaching for it, reaching for it and her knee was touching his. He could smell her hair; she was staring at his lips.

She's gonna kiss me, he thought, *she wants to kiss me.*

Just then Icabus started screaming.

It was awful screaming. Not human. A demon machine screaming. Icabus should not have been able to scream that loud at his age. And he screamed without taking a breath. The women sat scared, not knowing what to do as Morris ran towards Icabus. With his head thrown back and his fists locked to his legs, Icabus screamed in horror. Morris tried to figure what was wrong. Icabus looked at the women in disbelief, only to scream even louder. He saw something in the women that scared him. Icabus looked at Morris and screamed in his face. Icabus was so scared, so childlike in his fear that it scared Morris.

"Icabus, what is it? Tell me. It's Morris."

Then, from something inside him, Morris understood what was happening. What Icabus was seeing wasn't in the room. Morris somehow understood that to Icabus, Morris appeared as something roaring toward him with rabbit teeth and a goat's face. To Icabus, Morris had the hindquarter of a sick caribou, with catgut and pus for meat. He had the trunk and torso of a bear and the hands of a bleeding woman. The hair over his goat's face was black and dirty, like the tail of a dead horse. Morris knew to stand still with this vision and talk his friend down. Icabus stood back. He looked small and shriveled, like an old monkey.

"Icabus," Morris said, "listen to me. What you're seeing is not real. Someone has put a curse on you. Stand still. Stay still. The women will leave. I am here. I am here for you, Icabus. Don't be scared. On my honor, you can trust me."

They've taken his eyes, Morris thought. He wanted to slap Icabus for being so pitiful and hug him at the same time. Icabus looked from Morris' eyes back to the women and started screaming again. Morris looked at the women. They approached him, pulling their skins off. Underneath, they were skinned bears, peeling their mouths back, waiting to bite. Morris saw what Icabus saw. He started screaming with the old man.

Wake up! A voice told him. *Wake up! This is too much. This is too strong. Wake up, Morris!*

The curse was spreading like a virus to him.

Morris shot awake and could still hear Icabus screaming. *Where was he?* He saw the white canvas of the tent and the tent frame around him. He could hear the waves wash up the beach. Icabus' foamy and sleeping bag were there, but the old man was gone.

"Talking with the bushmen, I guess," Morris shivered and pulled his blankets closer. He didn't like that idea and wondered if the bushmen could wade through the Slave, out to the islands.

Oh, Icabus, Morris ached—*my teacher, my friend*.

"You sure got a lot of strength," Icabus said one time, passing him a cup of tea, "but you got no power. There's a difference."

"So how do I get both?"

"Hang with the boss here and I'll have you farting through silk."

They both burst out laughing.

Morris remembered the night he got off work and met Icabus coming from checking his nets. Icabus had given him a bag of whitefish and Morris was pleased. They walked over to Icabus' place only to find

Connie, Icabus' daughter, playing cards for money with three other women. The radio was blaring; the TV was on. Kids were sleeping on the floor and couch. One of the babies reeked and needed a change. Another was crying. The women kept playing, even after they were broke.

Icabus yelled as he swept the cards off the table. "I told you never to play cards on the supper table. Cards are the devil's work!"

Connie shot up and yelled, "Devil shit!" right to his face. The women picked up the cards and the kids. They took the game elsewhere.

Icabus stood rooted to the same spot and shook his head. Morris walked in. Icabus glanced at him. "She's getting snaky these days."

Morris studied Icabus a moment. "Pretty good lookin' snake."

Icabus looked at him and cracked the first smile. "You're okay, Metis," he said. "The wolf is strong in you."

When Morris threw back his head and laughed, he realized that had been the happiest he had ever been: he had just found Sheila and things were growing between them; he had the trust of Icabus; and he still had his hard-ons.

Then everything changed again. Everything.

Icabus had left for Edmonton to be with his daughter, Augustine, but had died in a mall. The coroner said it was age but Morris knew it was medicine. *Inkwo*. A killing prayer.

Morris had been watching the phones at the detachment while Jody Black Duck went for lunch. He was trying to call Augustine in Edmonton for more information on Icabus' death when three Cree women came in to make a complaint.

"Who's in charge here?" the fat one asked. She looked mean and her skin was the color of dead fish-eggs.

Morris stood up. "I am."

"You're not a Sergeant," the other one said, eyeing his uniform and his crotch.

"He's in Yellowknife," Morris stated.

"You'll do," the other stared at him. Her eyes were so brown they were black. "We have a complaint to make."

She has mean eyes, he thought. "Okay," he said, approaching the foyer. "What happened?"

He was reaching for his pen, pulling it out of his breast pocket when he felt something.

(Hey Hey Whatcha Doin'?)

He felt cold eager fingers going through his mind, like a Rolodex. He went back to the moment with Icabus; he went back to the fire they lit. He could smell the sting of sweet sulfur as Icabus struck the match; Morris could see the hair in Icabus' ears. He could see the burnt caterpillars landing on the prayer tobacco they were laying out. Morris went back to the exact moment, the exact millisecond it all began. He was aware he was screaming.

"He knows," one of the women said.

"Told you," the other agreed. "Those boys were right."

And he came full force back to the moment.

Morris came back down into his body. He smashed back over the desk, spilling pens and paper all over the floor. "Get the fuck outta my head!" he screamed, "Jody—anyone!"

They watched. The sisters watched.

"Who the fuck—how did?"

And it happened again. He went back to when he was in his kitchen. Those cold fingers were hotter, faster, deeper. They took him back to the moment in his kitchen when he savored the words that Icabus threw: *It starts tonight.*

He blacked out.

When he came to, Jody and her sweet tits were hugging his face, pulling his face into her warm chest yelling, "Constable! Wake up! What happened?"

He remembered playing possum a few seconds longer than he should have to feel her breasts pressed full into his face.

"Morris?"

That night, as he sat on the can, he felt it. It was on the base of his scrotum. At first he scratched oddly at it and then he pulled. A snake scale? Why was it black? He realized what was happening.

"Jesus!" he screamed. "They put medicine on me!"

44.

Stars.

The stars were out like a diamond splashboard in the sky. To his left, Morris could see the three stars of Orion's belt. Orion. The hunted.

Icabus, he and Icabus—

Lightning flashed in the south. In winter? Sheet lightning in winter?

Morris stared ahead, sipped his cold coffee and placed his cup on the dashboard. His hand was covered by a child's hand as the wind whistled through the window.

Lizard skin, he thought. Someone laughed in his ear.

Morris was suddenly aware of children playing in the back of his truck, peeling back his tarp, jumping on his cargo, peeking in the window. With swollen burnt fingers, they pulled and pried the glass on the passenger window down.

"Hey," Morris tried. "Hey —"

They began crawling into the cab of his truck with the cold winter air.

Morris turned, jarred awake by the heavy, ripe scent of burnt meat around him. A child's charred face smiled at him while another child's hand held his face and whispered to him in a language from Hell.

Morris listened, saw the black chalice of the child's mouth open and a black tongue slide out.

With ice-eaten fingers, a small boy held Morris' ears.

Morris swallowed a tongue that was colder than any snow.

Hey hey whatcha doin'?

My Fifth Step

This is my fifth step. I miss you. I'm sorry. I miss you and I'm sorry.

Do you think about me sometimes? I sure think about you. I think the hard feelings between us would go away if we just went for coffee sometime, just to check up on each other and see that the wounds weren't so deep anymore, but I don't think that will happen.

You'll always be with me you know. No matter what. What we had was good and I'm sorry for any bad between us. Really I am.

I think about you mostly when I'm around fire or when I hear a sad song. I start to feel hollow and I have to turn away. I look away and remember the nights we shared, the laughter — there was laughter. Remember? Before the battles, before the pissing contests between us about who was hurt more, who had done more, who had lied and betrayed more.

I'd love to see you again in the best way, your way. No power, no overwhelmance, no control, just a soft hug and a smile. I'd love to hear how you're doing and where you've gone. I'd love to watch you talk about your friends, your job, your boss, what you do alone, where you go to gather strength. Do you still love to swim? Do you have children? Is he good to you?

I was thinking the other day on a long drive with all my nephews and nieces that all we have — really have in this life — is our family and friends, and I'm glad you and I had some time together. I hope all your dreams come true — I really do. Lord knows, you deserve all good things that come your way.

Have I softened over the years? Well, for one, I quit fighting. I don't got the poop anymore, and, really, I can talk anyone down, and I think folks know I play for keeps so if you want to go, you're taking on a bull (in the sheets and in a fight ha ha!). So, I quit all that. Assholes are assholes. Lord knows it's not my job to bust'em or try to change 'em. There's man's way and there's God's way and I have learned to let go. I don't think I told you I love you the way you should have heard it. Sure, I said it when things were going good, but when things soured I never said it when you needed to hear it most, or maybe when I need- ed to. I'm sorry about that. I thought crying was a weakness, but I know now that it's a strength and that it takes something I always wanted: courage.

It's funny and sad but you said you never really got to know me all those years, but if you think about it I showed you more than anyone who I really am. When I brought you to the field behind the highway, I was showing you the innocence inside me, the place that's me, and when I took you to the lake, I was showing you the possibili- ties inside me, the freedom I feel all the time, and when I let you meet my grandparents, I was showing you the royalty of my family, the rich- ness of my blood and what we could share if we had a baby. Remember when I showed you how to call the northern lights? I hope you teach that to your children one night and that you tell them "a great man taught me this many moons ago."

I was surprised when you used how I communicate against me. Men are single-minded and women are emotional and can do way more at once. This is how we help and balance one another. You want- ed me to cry with you and I don't know any man who would or even could. You said I was capable of two emotions: anger and happiness, but that wasn't true either. I felt every emotion possible. Couldn't you read it in my eyes or hear it in my voice? My silence was never anger. It was meditation on everything you said, and sometimes I needed more time to answer than you would give me.

Courage. I have it now because I did go for counseling. When you left, you took the two most sacred words I know with you: HOME and FAMILY. That's why I got so crazy and that's why I never came back. The man inside me felt betrayed. The little boy inside me felt abandoned. The elder inside me was heartbroken with all the dreams I had for us. My spirit split when you left and it took oh about four years to get back to me. I fell down. Sure I did. I'm not going to talk about it but some of the rumors about me are true...I know about shame and doubt and embarrassment, but I'm a better man for it. I am more compassionate now, more giving, not willing to judge (try not to!). I give freely and have learned that the joy is in the giving. I treasure my friends and family every chance I get. "Affirmations are friends." It's true! There is help out there if you ask and look for it.

We're both so bloody proud and stubborn, and that was our downfall. I'm sorry family got involved on both sides and I'm sorry this town can be so cruel with its talk. We were the flavor of the month and things got out of control so fast. People need things to gossip about so they don't have to look at their own lives. They feed on misery to feel better about where they're at and we should have worked things out together—away from town. We should have gone camping for as long as we needed together. The land would have welcomed us home.

You'll never guess it but I'm softer now. Yeah, I love country music (now I know we'll never get back together — just kidding!). Well, maybe you like it now too. Yeah, it calms me, makes me feel. I'm actually a good little two stepper. I learned how at treatment and two steppin's where I got my wings back. Remember how I used to groan about how much cocoa butter you used on your feet at night? Well, I have a confession. Sometimes, when the day's been hard or I'm lonesome, I have some and I rub it on my feet and I wear my softest shirt and I fall asleep right away. I also remember how you used to take baths at night. Well, I do that too now and I wish I would have said yes to you every time you asked me to join you. I can't, for the life of me, imagine why I would have said no all those years.

Anyhow, I called your place a few times but some guy keeps answering. The fifth step teaches that if you think you may get someone in trouble or beat up by contacting them, then it's okay not to, but I figured that if I sent this here and it got published it would somehow find its way to you and you'd know that it was me and you'd know I was sorry.

I pray to God you're not getting hit or pushed around. There was this one elder at the lodge who said, "When a man hits a woman, he breaks something not even God can fix." He's right. I may have swore. I may have yelled, but I never hit and I never will. I'm proud of that.

I loved the way you pulled me into the tea dance every time. I waited for it. I loved the way you led me into the bush when I first came back to town. You saved my life that night. I loved making love to you and I miss your cooking. Most of all, though, I miss how when we slept together, you wrapped your arms around me and never let go. I never thanked you enough for all you did for me and I want to thank you for trusting me when we first met. You never held back and I did, and I never wanted to become the biggest disappointment in your life. I loved my coffee in the mornin', and I loved you in the afternoon…

remember that? I also miss listening to you talk in your sleep and making you smile with a joke or a story or just a look between us. You have such pretty eyes...

My family still asks about you, and I tell them you're happy and doing what gives you the most joy. I hope I'm right. I also hope whoever that guy is who answers your phone knows what a queen you are.

Take care of yourself and thank you again for all your love. You made me feel so special. I'm a better man because of you and I know now what's possible. Be gentle with yourself, my friend...now and forever... I miss your love and friendship...

Walk in beauty...

How I Saved Christmas

Things to do today:

Get laid

Wake up Clarence

Make better friends with the BJS!

Go to dentist

Go to drum dance

Well, I'm just groovy. Believe it. I'm in shop right now, finishing off a ring. It's simple really, how it's done. You take a hollowed out aluminum rod and you saw off an inch from the end and you buff it, sand it, shine 'er up and that's it. The shop teacher, Koala Mercier, is a burn out. Mostly we just leave him alone cuz we know he's about three months away from his pension.

He says my ring is by far the best. I engraved "S.O.P." on the ring in cool gothic letters. "S.O.P" stands for "Soldier of Passion." The chalkboard reads: "ONLY 14 MORE WELDING DAYS BEFORE CHRISTMAS!" and I have to get out of this town: my moshing is at an all time high and my soul right now is a caved-in dog cage. But enough about me.

See, I'm writing lots these days and I'm really hoping it'll take me places. I hand all the finished products to my new English teacher, Mr. Ron, who truly believes in me. He says I should explore other media and that I got what it takes. Oh yeah, I should tell you: I got stabbed in the back as well. See, when I hand in my stories, they're pretty Barbara Psychedelica and I got assigned to a counselor.

His name is Mr. Williams. He has pens and posters in his office that read, "THEY HAVEN'T BUILT AN AX THAT CAN CHOP DOWN A DREAM." He tries and all. I just can't get into it. He talks about Maslow's hierarchy of needs and priorities and setting goals while I look out the window to the far surrendered sky. It's sad really. But what can you do?

All I know is, I went into the bathroom, right outside his classroom and wrote on the wall "Last Chance For Doggy Style — 200 Meters". And I signed it: "Mister Williams, Guidance Counselor Extrordinaire." Then I added: "God Bless the BJS!"

The new English teacher, Mr. Ron, says if I can do prose, a play, some poetry, and fiction, I'll be able to get into this writing school down south. You'd swear my teacher has nocturnal emissions about my potential because he's already called and requested pamphlets. Here is an example of the poetry I've done so far:

Girls
Double jointed
Best spellers around
Always remember birth dates
Want to know your middle name!

Groovy, hey? That was written for this babe called Dedrie Meddows who has chrome submission tits. All I know is I ended up in Clarence's bathroom playing rock paper scissors with him for the best condoms. Clarence got the Crown and scored his first cousin. That was the night we were stoned on shrooms spitting apple juice at each other. It was sloppy lumberjack magic and I got to listen to Clarence's ass hydraulics slap his wet playdough balls off her ass for an hour. They sounded like this: slap! slap! slap!

When I fooled around with Dedrie, she kept asking, "What are you thinking? What are you thinking?"

I was just so amazed with her full, high, self-supporting breasts and hollow head nipples, I cried with delight: "Look at them biscuits! Look at them biscuits!"

"Don't make it dirty!" She cried back and pushed me away.

And I, under the Jesus Cameras, could not perform.

"Go," she said. "Just go."

"Well could we spoon?" I asked. Banished, I ended up doing a black-out dance with a sock around my neck. An hour later, Lila showed up and I'm talking straight funkadelic.

So here's two little quickies that can sum up my winter so far:

Video Games
If you kill these men
you can touch this woman

Pornos
The gentle things
they shove into each other

Which reminds me. It's 3:30. Almost home time. I have to look at my list:

Things to do today:
Get laid
Wake up Clarence

Make better friends with the BJS!

Go to dentist

Go to drum dance

"Gentlemen!" Koala calls out from his office, "if your work stations are clean, you may leave!"

BRRRRRRRRRRRRRRRRR!!

That's the buzzer. I grab my parky and pull on my Kamiks. It's time to wake up Clarence.

God really worked it out this year: Christmas is gonna be on a Sunday and New Year's Eve is gonna be on a Saturday. It's the coldest day of the year by the way: minus 45 degrees. That's not including wind or A-hole factor. You may have heard of the SAD syndrome. I think it's "Sloppy Lumberjacks and Depression" or somethin', but what it boils down to is a lack of light: Death by darkness. We are humans but we are also plants, and if a plant cannot get enough light, it cannot grow. Simple. When humans can't get enough light, they swallow shotgun barrels and pull triggers. That's my buddy Clarence if I'm not careful.

The good thing about it being minus 45 degrees is that the sunrise is spectacular. It's a Physics 30 orgasm. The light from the sun, which is low to the horizon, hits the ice-fog which hangs over this little northern town and you have rarefaction, refraction and some fancy light that makes you ache. Too bad you can't enjoy it without your cheeks splitting, it's that cold. And you would not bleed blood, either. You would bleed purple purple steam.

And something else: the snow here is as white as the milk of apples and the trees look like snapshot explosions. Wow, hey?

Dogs

Let's talk about 'em! I finally figured out why they're on this planet. They are the Jesus Cameras. What they see, Jesus and all the angels see. If you're smoking up with Nostradamus, for example, he'd be quite a party pooper. He'd be droning on and on a little like this:

NOSTRADAMUS: "You guys are dead. You're so dead. Millenium, baby. Get ready. Bombs. Fire. Cannibals. Cockroaches. One from the lesser tribes will acquire arms and toast your ass."

ME (AMBASSADOR OF LOVE): "Hey, Nos, quit hogging the hooka and shut your mouth, bee-otch!"

Anyways, the point is that if you were smoking up and you were on parole and a dog was in the room, it would really be Jesus and all the angels watching. That's the scoop, Jupe! And cats are Devil Cameras; they're Satan's little helpers. From their eyes, Satan and all his minions watch with drooling lips. And now you know why dogs and cats hate each other. The light and darkness war continues!

The BJS

I guess I should divulge the best kept secret in Simmer: The Blow Job Specialist! I don't know where she learned her oral techniques, but I sat at the base of Clarence's steps one night listening to him get a "Cosmic Blowjob" (his words) from her. I don't know if she took both of his jobbles in her mouth and sucked at the same time; I don't know if she stroked his prostate with her longest finger; I don't know what she did but he was wailing like a horse lit on fire. He still can't talk about what she did without twitches and spasms. All I know is he slept for days after and the BJS had vanished long before he woke up.

She isn't the prettiest girl in town, and I think that's why she had to go beyond the norm. Who taught her? Porn? Who?

Eight months black for slaves

Did I tell you I woke up to the sound of sizzling hash between the blades of squeezing knives? My Uncle Franky, a good man with a dependency problem, was hooting away and rolling fatties. No breakfast! Not even coffee! Just some black hash for a broken god seeking collision.

"Mornin'," I said as I got up and jumped into some long johns. "Howshegoin?"

"Pretty purple," my uncle said, meaning "hazy." "Jed and I were up 'til two last night making Grizzly patties for this catering gig he got for the drum dance."

I watched Uncle Frank brace for the smoke.

"Wanna know what?" He hooted. "Clarence (hoot) lost his birthday money to Tarvis last (hoot) night (hoot) at the bar."

"Fuck sakes," I said. "That damn Clarence."

Before I was out the door, my Uncle coughed, "Sal Bright (hoot hoot) don't wanna be Santa no more!"

But I didn't listen. I had to get to my sweet ass to school.

Clarence

Now let's take a look at how the eight month winter of the NWT affects mammals. Let's start off with Clarence Jarome who I have known since I moved here. After I lost rock-paper-scissors to him for the Crown condom, we kind of looked at this little bottle of baby oil on the sink, and I asked, "Well, should we play for it?"

Hell yes! We played best out of three and I lost, I lost, I lost. That party was absolute monkey house trauma. We had Slayer, D.R.I., Monster Magnet and Danzig on CD shuffle. I was a sunshine cannibal moshing it up in my toque and mukluks.

"I didn't know you were a thrasher," Lila smiled, standing there in her bizarre purple sweater and her sweet little ABBA shoes. I danced, sized her up, looked into her mouth and thought YES!

Clarence yelled. "Play Slayer's 'Mandatory Suicide!'"

Oh how we moshed. No Pink Floyd please. No Jimmy H. Just some kick ass hard core. To make a long story short: I had to stick handle around Lila's Jackie Chan boyfriend who was selling "White Widow" out of his I-ROC. He left to make the deal of the century and I took full hunger advantage. Slap, slap, slap...

This was a great year for the alternative lifestyle by the way: Great porn courtesy of Andrew Blake, great music courtesy of Napster, and I've just made friends with the BJS.

But enough about that. Let's get back to the quest.

Clarence had a tape of mine, which I stole off Eric. Eric and Clarence aren't speaking to each other anymore cuz Clarence puked on Eric's back. Such is life!

Here's who Eric puts on his tapes: The Cranes, The Prodigy, Afghan Whigs, Dead Can Dance, Slowdive, Siouxsie and the Banshees, Kate Bush, Jonathan Richman and The Modern Lovers. The best the best the best!

He calls this tape "The Grinder" and I'll need it as I nurture the sacred bond between the BJS and moi.

Anyways, I ran over to Clarence Manor cuz I'm his human alarm clock. He's kind of depressed lately and Prozac lets him sleep fourteen hours straight. It was his birthday yesterday. It even said so on the green screen. His house is across the potato field and I froze my ass off—even with added protection like woollies and long johns. I pulled my toque all the away down so I could see through the wool mesh and still I froze. Nobody on the streets but me. No parka queens to wave to. Eyes so cold they water. Snow piled high like thick, white mattresses, burying the hoods of trucks. It's like walking into a frozen marshmallow. Everything outside was so suddenly still and the air hung like a pregnant moose. One false move and the trees would shatter.

There was Clarence's house. I let myself in.

Clarence, as usual, was in his coma deep sleep. He's on pogey and doesn't have to work.

"Mono Boy!" I called as I barreled up the stairs. No answer, the chronic. Man, I swear Clarence was born tired.

"Lost your money last night, hey?" I threw his gonchies from the floor to his face.

"What!" Clarence sat up. "How the hell do people know these things?"

"Just do, now where's my tape—what the...?"

Something had changed about his room. It was still a mess with his CDs and tapes piled all over the place. He had posters up of Morrissey, The Cure and The Smiths. There were also pictures of Bat Girl all over the place with loving attention on her latex ass. His laundry basket was overflowing and my porno mags were fanned out all over his floor. What the hell? There were bullet holes in the walls!

There were about 20 bullet holes peppered all over the far walls and ceiling. It was his .22 caliber AR-7 survival rifle that he cradled in his arms. He had his banana clip, which meant he was capable of 33 semi-automatic shots as fast as he could pull the trigger. I won't go hunting anymore with him because of that gun.

"I thought you sold that," I said.

He looked at me. "Your tape is on the top shelf, by the shotgun. Now who the hell told you?"

"Clarence," I said, "what the hell happened here last night?"

"Spiders. I hear them in the walls."

I stared at him, hard.

"I know I know. I gotta get outta this town."

I looked for my tape. He pulled on his Sisters of Mercy T-shirt. "I swear to God this house is haunted. I gotta get out of here."

I found the tape. "Gretzky!" I put it in his ghetto and played it. It was Jonathan Richman and the Modern Lovers: "I go to bakeries all day long; there's a lack of sweetness in my life..."

"Lare!" he ran his hands through his hair. "Last night I turned 21. It's almost Christmas. I looked around, I looked at my friends and I just wanted to cry. I gotta get a job. I miss it. Oh God, I miss working."

I turned it down. "Give it time."

"Time? I don't got time! You know how close I came to pulling the trigger last night?"

I stuck my finger in one of the bullet holes. "Not worth it, man. Besides, who will the spiders play with?"

"I walked around the bar," he continued. "Yelling across the tables made me deaf, so I danced on the floor all by myself. I looked at the moose and caribou heads above the bar with their mouths open. I just walked up to them and said I was sorry. Somebody stuck red pool balls in the eye sockets of the buffalo skulls. I saw all the fish mounted on the walls, those big pikes and whitefish. I just walked up and said I was sorry. I poured beer in their mouths and got kicked out. On my birthday! It's Christmas for chrissakes." He paused. "I seen Sal Bright there. He don't wanna be Santa anymore."

"Look," I held out my hand. "We're making a deal right now. We won't deal with lotteries under 30 million."

"30 million!"

"Yeah," I grinned, "cuz we're worth it."

"Can't do it, man. There's a bingo in Hay River next week."

"Clarence," I said, "God won't give us this forever."

"What?"

"God gave us today and I'm gonna use it. I'm going. Don't forget about the drum dance tonight."

"Where?"

"Friendship Centre. Eight o'clock."

"Let's have a coffee," he said. "Then we'll play crib."

"No time, partner!" I said. "I got my tape, now I gotta see Eichman!"

"Eichman? Jesus! Isn't he secretly the lead singer for Rammstein? Hey! Don't you wanna hear how I lost my birthday money?"

"Naw," I got up. "You did it last year and you'll probably do it again next year—"

"But Larry!"

"Sol later, man!" I yelled. "Happy Birthday!"

That's what I did in front of the Jesus Cameras and everyone: Tough love, baby!

"I deserve to be loved by a beautiful and intelligent woman," I said to myself as I made a break for it. "I deserve to be loved by a beautiful and intelligent woman."

It was so cold out I cut through the old folk's home. Here the elders had all this tinsel and Christmas propaganda happening around them and they looked sad. Some of them were reading the paper and shaking their heads. Man, the old people in this town smoke like chimneys. Crazy coots!

On To Eichman

I gotta tell you about the dentist here. He's cold: a true technician of terror and torture. He's the type of guy who probably laughed when Old Yeller took a bullet in the head. Anyways, I walked into his chop shop and somebody had been hard at'er decorating the place for Christmas. There was music coming from the office and, sure enough, it was Bony M singing "Faleece Navee Datt!!" along with the punishing sound of a drill from the operating room, there was a coffee machine hissing out a fresh pot. There were charts all over the wall saying, "Gum Disease: prevention is the key."

The whole place smelled like cinnamon slaughter. There was a pile of Reader's Digests in a pile on a coffee table. I sat down on the couch. Over to the far left, under the coat rack, and beside the coffee machine, was a pair of white Kamiks standing in a puddle. Above them were parkas and a pair of big-ass caribou mitts. There was this little kid there, looking at me. Beside him sat his dad. The kid was reading a book. I poured a cup. My hands were a bruised purple. I'm surprised they just didn't seize. There was the latest Slave River Journal and the cover reported: "Sal Bright will no longer be Santa!"

What the!?—I picked it up and read it.

His quote: "Due to the politics, I cannot remain true to the cause. If I spend too much time in Indian Village, the Metis get mad at me; if I spend too much time near the church, the Dene get mad; if I don't spread myself around, the non-Natives get mad and that isn't what Christmas is about. Besides, why not have someone else give it a try?"

The article went on and on. I couldn't believe it. That's what my uncle and Clarence were talking about. That's why the elders were shaking their heads and looking sad. I was going to steal the article to read later but a woman came out of the operating room looking pale and wobbly. Half her face was falling off by the look of it.

"Hullo," I said and took off my jacket.

"Honey," the father greeted.

"Mum, can I have some ice cream?" the little guy asked.

She said, "Asha Ukka Ukka!"

Her face was so frozen!

"Are you okay? Here's your jacket." Her husband said. She looked wasted. From behind her came Eichman himself. "Next week, Barbara. Ten o'clock, Tuesday?"

Barbara turned around and floppily waved at him, kind of groggy like, and kept rambling, "Alsha Ulsha Uka Uka."

The family left. Eichman stared after them, smiling. I could hear his assistant washing up for me. I heard from the scurvy dogs in the high school that she was a sweet little honey who didn't drink or go out at all. The first week she got here, the meat hooks were out. Guys got all dressed up and cruised in their trucks doing a smoke show at the four-way by spinning out. When she went to do her shopping at the Bay, all the packing boys tripped on their dicks rushing to be the one to pack for her. Clarence said the boys were being shot down on all fronts and they were too devastated to call a retreat. And now I'd have my moment in the sun—with what? A damn drill in my mouth and a needle sliding through my gums.

"Larry Sole?" she called out. Eichman was still staring off as Barbara and her fam wobbled through the snow.

"C'est moi," I said and hung up my jacket.

First I saw the hair, then her bust which heaved like war cannons under her lily white suit. What a presence! I looked at her slim trim tummy and bet she had a six pack. I sat down on the seat. Sure I did. It had this rattly white paper that wrinkled and crackled whenever I moved. I was getting settled when she came from the office with a file. Wow! A brunette with straight hair tied in a bun. She was trying to be professional and all by tying this bib around me, but she had to lean her chest near my face and I wanted to snap my teeth and hang on like a wolverine.

Eichman came in and looked at a file she handed him. I leaned over and checked out the feet. Moccasins! The beadwork didn't look Dogrib, Slavey or Chipewyan. Where was she from?

Eichman perused my file, probably plotting the best routes for attack and carnage. Ever since I can remember, Eichman had this one poster on the damn ceiling. It's this witch with a warty nose and most of her teeth are missing. The tooth stubs she does have left are black and yellow. She's green and spooky and she's holding a lollypop as big as your ass. She's asking, "Care for some candy, my sweet?"

And in the back of her, there's more candy and mountains of lollypops. I remember we were talking one day at school, me and the boys. We all agreed this poster has created more nightmares, more trauma, more scorched shorts than The Exorcist. I mean, what kind of sick bastard puts up that kind of poster for children, elders and expecting moms to look at while he solders their teeth shut or slices into their gums?

"When was your last check up?" Eichman asked.

"Six months ago," I lied.

"Bite on this," he said and put something in my mouth that bit with plastic teeth into my gums. He aimed a magnificent rifle at my face, near my cheek and I checked out the Dene honey as she put this heavy blanky on me. A heart shaped ass. Sweet! Sweet!

The blankey was lead insulated, I guess, with a big flap meant for genitalia. The way she was putting it on was like she was tucking me in and I was tempted to say, "Night, Mommy," but, instead, being Big Daddy Love and all, I leaned forward and sniffed her hair and she smelt like something blue and lush and bright, like the water children are baptized with.

"Where you're from?" I asked.

"Hold still!" Eichman ordered and felt my cheeks.

"Deline'," she said darting her eyes between Eichman and I. Nervous, I guess, cuz she was working.

"You know Jed?" I asked. He was from Franklin.

"Jed!" she beamed, "Yes I do! Where is he?"

"Cember, please," Eichman said, meaning "Shut up," and to me: "Will you hold still?"

"He's going out with my mom. He'll be at the drum dance tonight. He's doing the catering."

Eichman man-handled me into silence. Can you believe it? What a power freak. There was the crinkle of the paper beneath me, and my feet were getting hot as I still had on my boots and woollies. The scent of a cinnamon death soaked into my clothes and skin, suffocating the small mouths of my pores. He and Cember left the room. I heard, "Clear" and the magnificent rifle went "Brr" and that was it. I looked up to the old hag with the crumbling teeth gurgling. "Care for some candy, my sweet?"

"Open," Eichman said and held out his white-gloved hand. With my white froth cow tongue, I pushed it out and there was a stringy slug trail of spit, which he lassoed around the plastic blade. He handed it to Cember who took it and left the room. He put the plastic blade on the other side and did the whole process again.

I stared into the mouth of the hag on the ceiling and plotted erogenous camera mischief: (Me, Cember: slap! slap! slap!)

When Eichman and Cember were finished, they whispered tiny black secrets back and forth. I started thinking about Sal Bright, Simmer's Santa. He just had to be Santa this year. For as long as I can remember, he would always dress up and have his wife pull him on a sleigh with their car. He'd crank up a huge generator for the thousands of lights and blaring music to announce Santa's arrival on your street. It was like the hand of God when he appeared. The lights, the music, the magic of it all with him waving and smiling.

You could always hear him "HO HO HO'ing" all over town through his megaphone and the dogs would howl and chase him like some parade of beast demons trying to tear a holy man down. Kids would all run up to their windows and wave like convicts. Even parents shoveling their driveways would wipe their runny noses on the back of their woolly mitts and smile.

If he wasn't Santa this year, the whole damn thing wouldn't work. I knew it. Even if I was a preaching hypocrite most of the time and even if there would always be a "Care for some candy, my sweet?" poster up in the dentist's office, you just had to have Christmas to stretch out and wiggle your toes. There were 2,500 of us humans here in Simmer and the year had been so hard with all the lay-off's and cutbacks.

Eichman stood above me. Cember sat beside me. He was gabbing on and on: "...cap has fallen out and we'll put it back on for you."

I guess I was thinking so hard I didn't notice Eichman was already greasing up a Q-tip with some paste and squeezing my cheeks together so I'd open up.

"We've also found a small cavity on your..."

"Aw who cares," I thought. "Do your job, eh? You're going to hurt me either way."

It never failed. Every time I came in, I knew I was gonna suffer. Eichman never failed to incinerate my central nervous system with a blade or needle. He swabbed my lower back gum and I looked at Cember.

"If anything happens, baby," I wanted to say, "tell 'em I cared. Tell 'em I was a bright light in a two dollar town."

So I took notes of everything that went on in my head while they drilled, sucked and needled my teeth and gums. Here it is and it's important that I document how the government and the dentists are taking out the Soldiers of Passion: I'm not going to change a damn word. You deserve the pure octane, unadulterated, calligraphy-on-Wednesdays truth. Here it is: "FASCIST ROOT KILLER! I HAVE THE HUGE WHITE EYES OF BISON BEFORE THE BULLET SPLITS THE SKULL

THEY MIGHT AS WELL BE STICKING A BARREL IN MY MOUTH I CAN'T
IT'S NOT NO FROZEN HURTS HURTS HURTS I'M A RATTLESNAKE MY
VENOM HE'S TRYING TO GET AT THE MAIN TRUNK NERVES THAT HAVE
FUNNELED AND TUNNELED INTO THE ROOT SYSTEM OF MY FACE OH
JESUS JESUS PLUCK ME YOUR BRIGHTEST FLOWER FROM THIS YOUR
TRAUMA GARDEN MY TONGUE THE NEEDLE COULD TAKE YOU SO EASILY
STINKY GLOVES NOW I'M DELIRIOUS TEN YEARS OF THERAPY AND I
MIGHT JUST MAKE IT I'M GURGLING BLOOD PLEASE STOP PLEASE STOP
THE WHITE PAIN FROM MY MOUTH EXPLODES BUTTERFLY SNOW FROM
IT FALLS I'M..."

"Care for some candy, my sweet?"

All done. They wiped their hands of cold medical slaughter. I
needed some water to gurgle the spit and blood. "Who," I thought, "who
has placed a burning stalk of rhubarb in my mouth?"

Eichman beamed. "You had quite the little nap."

Cember undid my bib and looked at me with her teardrop eyes.

"I deserve to be loved by a beautiful and intelligent woman," I
tried to say but alls that came out was: "Alsha alsha uka aka."

"Eeeeeezzzzyyy," she helped me get up. I wobbled out of the
room and there was somebody else waiting.

Floppily, I got my coat. Floppily, I looked at Cember and wove a
little kiss, which I summoned from my dry throat, past my swollen moose
lips, through my teeth towards her. But she looked away and was on to
other things.

"Too bad, baby," I thought, "we coulda' been good together..."

I practically fell down the stairs I was so weak. I pulled on
my mitts and toque. "Wait a minute," I thought. "Wait one rattlesnake
minute."

I turned around. Eichman was staring at me through his window, smiling.

I got the hell away.

I guess while me and my moose lips are walking home, and while I'm having my ears stung by a thousand invisible snow bees, I should tell you about me trying to get laid all the time. I'm really quite reckless about my sexuality, and I'm ready to rock any day of the week, but that's only because I'm a product of a lonely town. I mean this town is full of flatliners. A soul hits the ground here every seven seconds.

I realized last Tuesday how lonely I was and it hit me. Hard. So I put some condoms by my bed and I gave all my porno mags to Clarence. Some people have to walk off hangovers or bouts of fury; I have to walk off The Heat. With leather suit shoes through knee high snow, I walk, patrol, and search, led by the heavy eyes of hunger, looking for love. Damn this sexual peak! Damn it straight to hell!

This town. Home of the big diesels, big track pants and big bad booze faces. I know every inch of this cage and it's only getting smaller—and I refuse to play Bingo! Don't even get me started about Bingo. I want to kill that game! And come to think of it, when was the last time a woman seduced me? When was the last time someone spent hours plotting how to get me into the sack? When was the last time someone came up to me and said, "Larry, I think you're funnier than a French tickler! I think you're the only one who hasn't been on empty for the past three years!"

I mean, these topics have to be addressed.

And I'm a good lay. I'm officially a good lay. After all, my blood is loaded with Testosterone making my balls 340 twin overhead cams jacked to the nuts!

And this town doesn't help. They take with their teeth here. There should be a sign on the airport road that reads:

WELCOME TO FORT SIMMER
PUMPIN' CAPITAL OF THE NWT
IF WE CAN'T KNOCK YOU UP WE'LL KNOCK YOU OUT!

And when you leave this little hellhole, there should be a sign on the highway that says:

THANK YOU FOR VISITING
COME AGAIN
IF WE COULDN'T BREED YOU WE PROBABLY BEAT YOU!

Yes, yes, they may have labeled me a failure in physics; they may have called home because I have four lates, but they did not see me for the gift of spirit and breath that I am.

I went home. It was my turn to cook and I couldn't wait until the drum dance to eat. I wrote one outstanding poem thinking about the Old Folk's Home. It went like this:

The Breath Of Elders
The breath of elders
like the breath of elephants close
fear mouse and his dream
for mouse has the dream of flight above snow
and mouse has the nightmare of teeth and steel
and steel is the cage of dog
and dog is chained

dog wants pussy
pussy is eating its cold bald litter
and the litter bald has the dream of nipples
and nipples love the taste of teeth
and teeth are the embrace for cannibals
and cannibals have to eat their buddies
and buddies never talk of love
and love is a porno with the sound turned low
and low is the swoop from hawk to mouse
and earth has risen to taste rain's skin
as skin is a field of dying flowers
and flowers are felt like God's fine hands
as he steals and holds the breath of elders...

After I finished, I just sat in the hallway with my purple ears
defrosting from the sting of invisible snow bees. As the windows
fogged up, I could smell the caribou hamburger sizzling in its sauce
and in ten minutes the spaghetti would be ready. I kept thinking about
passion, about how it was the last clean thing I had. I started thinking
about how horribly pathetic this year would die if Sal Bright didn't play
Santa. What about the kids? What about the elders? What about guys
like Clarence or Uncle Frank? What about the community? What about
the government workers? Any minute, something in their backs could
blow. Even Eichman, what about him? I thought of all the seized metal
engines outside and the seized human engines inside. And I thought of
me. I needed it too. I guess I had a grand mal seizure about the
whole thing and decided it was up to me. I mean, didn't sometimes...
didn't you ever think that you were dead, that you were already

buried, but you were given one day to come back and make things right? One day—through the politics, lies and the sloppy lumberjack butchery, God's permission was yours to come back to bring light to the world and add another color to the rainbow?

No bullshit. This is how I saved Christmas on the coldest day of the year. I called Sal Bright up.

"Lo!" He called as he answered the phone.

"Hello, is this Sal Bright of Fort Simmer, Northwest Territories?"

"Yes it is."

"Sal, my name is Tarvis Marvin calling from Emmunton, Alberta."

"Zat right, eh?"

"Yes, Sir, and I represent the Canadian Council of Moments."

"The what?"

"Canadian Council of Moments. It's an international organization to honor and commemorate Soldiers of Passion."

"Izzat right?"

"Yessir, and, Sir, it is my sincere pleasure to award you with the Canadian Council of Moments Award."

"Oh?"

"Yessir and your name has also been put into this year's awards as well for your involvement as Santa Claus."

"Well," he breathed, "we might have a problem—"

"Sir," I interrupted, "I understand you are thinking of not being Santa this year."

"Yeah," he began, "see, we got so much politics here."

"I read."

"You did?"

"Yessir. We have eyes in the most unique places and we understand your feelings on this matter. That is why I decided to call you up myself and ask you—*no*—beg you to keep up the good work."

"Wow..."

"Yessir, we here at the Canadian Council of Moments have applauded your efforts from the very beginning and we are all holding our breath that you continue."

"Really?"

"Yessir, I want to tell you that you'll be receiving something very special in the mail."

"Oh?"

"Yes! A customized ring just for you that boasts 'S.O.P' for 'Soldier of Passion' and a thank you note from myself representing the council."

"Hey that's great!"

"You've earned it, Sir."

"Yeah, well, I guess I should tell you that it sure is wonderful being Santa."

"I bet!"

"Yeah, you see the kids and you see them waving and you know they might not get a thing for Christmas but you gave them this. You gave them something."

"I sure am glad you called," he continued. "I was thinking of taking the wife and kids up to Yellowknife for a break, but I think I'll stay. I just wish there wasn't politics."

"We know," I said. "We're only too aware of the situation and we sympathize with you."

"Thanks," he said. "Thanks a lot."

"So you'll do it?" I asked. "You'll be Santa?"

"Yes," he said. "Yes I will."

"Mahsi Cho!" I yelled. "Woo hoo! You'll get your ring in the mail, Sir. And we'll be watching you this Christmas!"

"You bet!" He yelled. "Hey, honey! Hey, kids! I'm gonna be Santa again!" and I heard a cheer from his family.

And I heard a cheer from me. I had found another Soldier of Passion. And that, dear brothers and sisters, is how I saved Christmas.

O-lay!

Afterwords

Mermaids

I received a call one night from a friend who owned a pub. Trika had put aside a twenty-dollar bill she found while cashing out. The bill was inscribed with the words: "My mother was cursed the day she bore me. I am faint with envy of the dead." The words were written with a child's red crayon and the handwriting was horrible. I knew I had to write about whoever wrote this and where they were when they did.

And I remembered that I had heard of a medicine man who could call the wind with a two-dollar bill, and I wondered what it would be like if whoever wrote on the twenty-dollar bill could meet this elder.

After "Mermaids" was written, CBC Radio One's Between the Covers bought it for their "Festival of Fiction" and I converted it into a radio play. The producer, Ann Jansen, asked who we could use for a voice actor to narrate Torchy's voice. Immediately, I knew: "Ben Cardinal."

I met Ben when I wrote for "North of 60." Ben is a force. You feel him before he enters a room. I was struck with his voice. It too is a force, and I thought Ben's voice could capture that "cough drops and whiskey" feel to a voice that was raised on a steady diet of tough times and stolen dreams. This story is for you, Ben, and for a little girl named Stephanie who stole my heart because she was so neglected.

I started this in my trailer in Fort Smith and finished it when I moved to Bella Bella, British Columbia.

As a radio play, Mermaids aired nationally on Wednesday, May 23, 1998. It was later published as the short story you see here in *skins: contemporary Indigenous writing* by Kegedonce and Jukurrpa Press in 2000.

If Torchy could sing a song, I would have to say it was "This Time" by The Verve off their *Urban Hymns* album. When I listen to this song, I keep seeing Torchy and Stephanie on that bus, laughing, riding into the sun together with nothing but hope and new dreams...I also think of Snowbird hugging his new granddaughter and crying with joy.

Let's Beat the Shit out of Herman Rosko!

I was at a dance one night in Fort Smith standing next to a man feared by the whole town. I was watching the dance floor. One guy (we'll call him "David Brown") was really shaking his ass and the ladies were loving him. It was his night and the other guys in the McDougal Centre weren't too happy about it. I grew up with David and was proud of him. He wasn't raised in the best way, but there he was: all dressed up, fresh from college, a new hairstyle, just giving it all he had. He'd come home a man.

I could feel the energy change from the guy I was standing beside. I could feel a rage and tension growing around him. So I said, to break the silence, "Hey, David's really going whole hog out there. Good stuff!"

"Ah fuck," this guy said. "He's a Brown; he'll always be a Brown. It don't make no difference."

I started thinking about how some folks in small towns can really grind someone down, so I wrote this one night in Victoria while I was going for my degree. "Let's Beat the Shit Out of Herman Rosko!" was originally published in The Inner Harbour Review (University of Victoria Press) in 1996. This is for "David" and for my brothers.

Why Ravens Smile to Little Old Ladies as They Walk By...
I heard a variation of this story on a fishing island outside of Edzo on the Great Slave Lake. We were at a science camp with a dozen kids, scientists and Dogrib elders. The lake dropped so fast one afternoon, we were stranded out there. We weren't expecting this at all, but it didn't matter. We had lots of grub, a full moon, a great fire, and a small army of great storytellers out there. I'm sorry if the story tricked you, but the raven is a trickster and I'm such a goddamned liar....

I wrote this in Yellowknife when I heard that Seventh Generation Press was looking for stories for an anthology. They published it in their anthology titled A Shade of Spring in 1999. This story is for James Croizier who has always been there for me and for my family.

The uranium leaking for rayrock mines and port radium is killing us
I visited a friend, Pam Warner, in Victoria, BC. She was renting a home that turned out to be very haunted. I felt it as soon as I walked into the house. It felt like people were screaming all around me but I couldn't see them or hear them. I could only feel the energy against me. What can I say? I was inspired and ended up running home and writing this in one sitting. I immediately called Pam back, but I got her answering machine. I guess I spooked her when I said, "I think

people were butchered here" and she ran away too! I wanted the spirits there to know I was on to them and I read this entire passage to them through the machine, so they'd leave me the hell alone when I went back. (I never did—Are you *fuckin'* nuts?)

For those of you who don't know, the Northwest Territories was home to the world's first uranium mine: Port Radium (1932–1960) located in Sahtu Dene territory. The uranium that was used by the US Government to develop the World War II Atom Bomb technology and ferocity behind the detonation over Hiroshima and Nagasaki came from a number of places: American and African mines and Port Radium. The US Government ordered 918 tonnes of uranium from Port Radium. Later, Uranium 2308 was harvested from Rayrock mines (1955–1957) in Dogrib territory in the NWT and was sold to Atomic Research of Canada. Despite the Canadian government's knowledge in 1931 and 1932 of the serious health hazards associated with exposure to the dust from high-grade radioactive ores, Dene men, referred to as "coolies," were used to transport the radioactive ore along the 2,100 kilometre route called the "Highway of the Atom" without health warnings. Many of the Dene workers later developed cancer. Additionally, 1.7 million tons of radioactive tailings were dumped into the Sahtu (Great Bear Lake) — the ninth largest lake in the world and home to the world's largest trout fishing.

I wanted to combine the raw emotion inspired by the haunted house with how horrified I am about these mines and the legacy they've left behind. This story was originally published in *Gatherings VII* in 1996 and later republished in *Gatherings X* (Theytus Books) in 1999. This story is dedicated to Cindy Kenny-Gilday who continues to advocate for the Sahtu Dene.

I narrated "the uranium leaking from rayrock and port radium mines is killing us" as a spoken word piece for Redwire Magazine's "Our Voice is Our Weapon and Our Bullets are the Truth" CD featured in their April 2003 (Vol. 5, No.4) issue.

Sources

"How Uranium from Great Bear Lake Ended up in A-Bombs: A Chronology" by Gordon Edwards, Ph.D. (You can find this article with any search engine on the Internet.)

"Feds to help Deline" by Terry Halifax (Northern News Services) www.nnsl.com/frames/newspapers/archive00-1/jan24_oohelp.html

"Deline demands action: Dene seek crisis assistance to deal with uranium fall out" by Glen Korstrom www.nnsl.com/frames/newspapers/archive98-1/mar30_98dene.html

"Digging up the facts: Deline uranium investigation coming" by Glen Korstrom www.nnsl.com/frames/newspapers/archive98-1/apr98/ apr20_98del.html

"Deline Dene dash to Japan" by Darren Campbell www.nnsl.com/frames/newspapers/archive98-1/aug98/aug3 _98japan.html

"Truth of the tailings: Feds agree to cleanup a radioactive legacy in the Sahtu" by Terry Halifax www.nnsl.com/frames/newspapers/archive99-2/oct25_99radium.html

"Deline takes message to Ottawa: Deline radiation message finally getting through" by Richard Gleeson www.nnsl.com/frames/newspapers/archive98-1/jun15_98radium.html

The Night Charles Bukowski Died

When I went for my degree at UVIC there was a horrible case of bullying and intimidation that occurred in our dorm. I ended up sticking up for a young guy who didn't have an aggressive bone in his body. He took what several guys dished out continuously, and I knew it was just a matter of time before the suicide spirit visited our dorm.

I had to move out because I couldn't afford the dorm any more. I also left with disgust because no one was doing anything about the bullying.

The day I moved out, I walked back to the dorm, snuck in, ran upstairs, and walked into the room of the chief instigator in the whole crisis. I threatened to blind him with a fork if he went after my young friend ever again.

"You can't threaten me," he said as his little chin just trembled away. "I'm going to report you. You'll be thrown outta here by the end of the day."

"I already moved, you dizzy shit," I said, "so I got nothing to lose." (Was that a tear in his right eye? It was a tear in his right eye!)

"Okay," he said. "Take it easy. I'll leave him alone."
That walk to my new home was the best walk of my life. The birds

were singing. Kids were playing. My little buddy was safe. That guy and his crew never went after my little buddy again.

I wrote this one night in my dorm room during the worst of the abuse and intimidation in our residence. I wanted it to read like a blur and capture how I felt and probably what might have happened if certain plans I'd been working on were executed. "The Night Charles Bukowski Died" was originally published by Theytus Books in *Gatherings XI* in 2000. CBC Radio broadcast "The Night Charles Bukowski Died" for "Between the Covers" as a radio drama in 2003, narrated by —you guessed it— Ben Cardinal. It's dedicated to Mark "Freddy Boom Boom" Paron and the men this story's about.

Sky Burial

I was with my best friend, Chris Paul, one afternoon in a mall in Victoria, BC. We were at a food court and I saw the most beautiful Native girl eating with a white lady. I watched them and it was apparent to me that this girl was a foster child and that this lady had taken her under her wing and there was a lot of respect, love and trust between them. I started thinking, "What if a dying medicine man saw her in the mall and gave her everything he had?"

I wrote it that evening in my new home in Victoria. This was after the bullying incident in my dorm. It was published in the anthology, *Blue Dawn, Red Earth*, edited by Clifford Trafzer, in 1996 (Dell Books). Good ol' Ben Cardinal narrated "Sky Burial" for CBC Radio in celebration of the Honouring Words Tour of Canada in October, 2002. This is dedicated to my mother, Rosa Wah-shee, and Chris Paul.

Snow White Nothing for Miles

The title for this story was inspired from the first line in "Driven like the snow" off the Sisters of Mercy's *Floodland* album.

When I was a child, I overheard my uncle Alexi tell my father not to ever stop on the road between Rae and Yellowknife because of the spirits who lingered there. I was terrified—and, wouldn't you know it? my mom (despite my pleas from the back seat) made my dad stop the truck for a smoke break along the haunted road! My childhood ended right there and I was convinced we had brought "others" into our home for years.

I grew up listening to stories about the ancient rivalry between the Crees and the Dogribs, and I wondered what would happen if that old warfare spirit was called back between us again. I wanted to use the sweatlodge to bring the two tribes together. I've heard of sweatlodges run for money, and I never agreed with it. Sweatlodges are not our family's way, and I was told not to participate in them by my grandfather because we have other medicine. I wrote this in Yellowknife after working outside of Rae-Edzo at Sah Naji Kwe. "Snow White Nothing for Miles" was originally published in *Rampike* (Summer, 2000). This story is for Dylan Vasas and Trevor Cameron.

My Fifth Step

A buddy of mine told me about his fifth step in the AA Program and how he so wanted to contact one of his ex's but couldn't. His reason, he told me, was that there is a sub-clause in this step. It says that, if by contacting someone you've hurt in your past you will put them in harm's way (usually by their present partner), you are allowed to not contact them to say you're sorry. I couldn't help but think of a lost love story and I took it from there. I wrote this one evening in Bella Bella and it's dedicated to everyone I have ever known. I am sorry…

How I Saved Christmas

After working as a Writer-Trainee with CBC Television's "North of 60," I ended up returning home to Fort Smith. I was lonely and starving with it. I was writing *The Lesser Blessed* and Larry, the main character, wanted to try something new, something away from the novel. Fort Smith was going through tough times economically and you could feel the town morale at its lowest. Well, Larry told me one night that he wanted to save Christmas.

Duncan MacPherson and his wife, Carol, had been the Fort Smith Christmas saviors for years. Duncan would dress up like Santa and his wife would drive him around town. They had this magnificent sleigh rigged up on a trailer and you could hear their sound system five miles away. I know there are entire continents in heaven reserved for the MacPherson family because of the joy they brought us all. I read one afternoon (at the height of my hunger) in the Slave River Journal that Duncan was going to retire and I burst into tears, so I wrote this as a prayer, and, thankfully, the MacPhersons stayed with it for a few more years.

This is for them and for Jon Liv Jaque who made those dark winter months glorious. I wrote this in my dad's basement in Fort Smith, and those were the salad days, baby!

Acknowledgments
The author gratefully acknowledges the financial support of the NWT Arts Council, Department of Education, Culture and Employment. With special thanks to Kateri Akiwenzie-Damm, Michael Bryson, and Grant Sheppard for editing this collection and believing. Thanks, as well, to everyone at the Slave River Journal, Tim Atherton, and Leslie Leong. Special thanks, as well, to Shannon Ludwig and everyone at Metropolis Records, especially their artists.

These stories were rewritten, remixed and remastered while listening to Tool, Project Pitchfork, Ikon, A Perfect Circle, Placebo, Radiohead, Slowdive, The Verve, PJ Harvey and the Cocteau Twins. Special thanks to Shannon Ludwig and everyone at Metropolis Records.

Mahsi
These stories were inspired by the lives, friendship and stories of Trevor Cameron and Janice Whiskeyjack, Trevor Evans, Chris Paul, Garth Prosper, Pam Warner, Cindy Blackstock, Chad Jobe, Glen and Leslie Douglas, Malcolm and Henry, Dylan Vasas, Marco de Hoogh, Eric Vorgaard, Jon Liv Jaque, James Croizier, Roger, Jamie and Johnny Van Camp, my parents: Rosa Wah-shee and Jack Van Camp, Roger Brunt, all the medicine people I have ever met, all my teachers (you know who you are), Mike, Sage, Raven, Jasmine, the En'owkin International School of Writing faculty (with special thanks to Jeannette Armstrong, Lee Maracle, Maurice Kenney, Donna Goodleaf, Beth Cuthand and Gerry William) and students, Theytus Books (with special thanks to Greg Young-Ing and Florene Belmore), the University of Victoria's faculty (with special thanks to Jack Hodgins, Smaro Kamboureli, Marilyn Bowering, and WD Valgardson) and everyone I went to school with. Thanks, as well, to Jennifer Naedzo, Edna, John Beder, Wayne Hussey, Nick Tosches, Donny Boxer, Trika MacDonald, Marty Ballantyne and Zoe Hopkins, Alec Lyne, Mike Mahauser, Ryan Klaschinsky, Jane Inyallie, Louise Spencer, Tiffany Midge, Irene Sanderson, Ken Shelton, Ron Klassen, Judith Drinnan, and George Littlechild. To everyone in Fort Smith and in memory of Joey Ramone. —— Mahsi cho!

Thank you for reading my stories and may the Creator
bless you now and always. Mahsi cho!